DEKOK AND THE NAKED LADY

"DeKok" Books by A.C. Baantjer:

Published in the United States:
Murder in Amsterdam
DeKok and the Sunday Strangler
DeKok and the Corpse on Christmas Eve
DeKok and the Somber Nude
DeKok and the Dead Harlequin
DeKok and the Sorrowing Tomcat
DeKok and the Disillusioned Corpse
DeKok and the Careful Killer
DeKok and the Romantic Murder
DeKok and the Dying Stroller
DeKok and the Corpse at the Church Wall
DeKok and the Dancing Death
DeKok and the Naked Lady
DeKok and Murder on the Menu

Available soon from InterContinental Publishing:
DeKok and the Brothers of the Easy Death
DeKok and the Deadly Accord
DeKok and Murder in Seance
DeKok and Murder in Ecstasy
DeKok and the Begging Death
DeKok and the Geese of Death
DeKok and Murder by Melody
DeKok and Death of a Clown
DeKok and Variations on Murder
DeKok and Murder by Installments
DeKok and Murder on Blood Mountain
DeKok and the Dead Lovers
DeKok and the Mask of Death
DeKok and the Corpse by Return
DeKok and Murder in Bronze
DeKok and the Deadly Warning
DeKok and Murder First Class
DeKok and the Vendetta
DeKok and Murder Depicted
DeKok and Dance Macabre
DeKok and the Disfiguring Death
DeKok and the Devil's Conspiracy
DeKok and the Duel at Night
and more . . .

*DeKok
and the
Naked Lady*

by
BAANTJER

translated from the Dutch by H.G. Smittenaar

INTERCONTINENTAL PUBLISHING

ISBN 1 881164 12 8

Printing History:
    1st Dutch printing: 1978
    2nd Dutch printing: 1978
    3rd Dutch printing: 1979
    4th Dutch printing: 1982
    5th Dutch printing: 1983
    6th Dutch printing: 1984
    7th Dutch printing: 1984
    8th Dutch printing: 1985
    9th Dutch printing: 1988
    10th Dutch printing: 1989
    11th Dutch printing: 1990
    12th Dutch printing: 1991
    13th Dutch printing: 1992
    14th Dutch printing: 1993

    1st American edition: 1994

Typography: Monica S. Rozier
Cover Photo: Peter Coene with thanks to H. van Gils Company

DeKok
and the
Naked Lady

Apologies to my faithful readers and fans. I don't usually have as many victims in one of my stories. But this is the twelfth DeKok novel and I thought that an even dozen corpses would not be out of place.

— *A.C. Baantjer*

1

Detective-Inspector DeKok of the Amsterdam Municipal Police (Homicide) was seated behind his desk in the large detective room of the ancient police station at Warmoes Street, at the edge of Amsterdam's Red Light District. He felt at peace with the world and leaned far back in his old-fashioned swivel chair, his legs comfortably stretched out on his desk and a happy smile on his face.

"The Commissaris," he said to his younger colleague, partner and friend, Vledder, "has expressed his appreciation."

Vledder grinned cynically.

"So," he said, "and exactly how did he express this appreciation?"

DeKok made vague gestures in the air above him.

"He spoke words of praise. Apparently it has finally come to his notice that we both were recently wounded in the pursuit of what is commonly referred to as our duty."

The young Inspector felt his upper arm where, a scant few weeks ago, he had been wounded by a bullet from a drug dealer. He looked at DeKok's hand where only an adhesive bandage reminded one of the severe bite DeKok had suffered when trying to arrest a young woman.

"And what," pursued Vledder, "would the Commissaris* have done if the bullet had been a few more inches to the left, or if you had died of blood poisoning? A human bite is the most infectious wound you can get, I always heard. What if we both had died?"

DeKok rubbed the bridge of his nose with a little finger.

"No doubt," he said placidly, "the Commissaris would have been kind enough to utter a few words of praise at our grave site."

"Sure, I can see it now. Motorcycles, band playing with muffled drums and with full military . . . eh, I guess police honor. What a farce."

"Perhaps," agreed DeKok, "but it's the politically correct thing to do, you see. The Commissaris is worried about his pension. It's the only thing that seems to occupy him lately . . . Bah."

Vledder looked up in surprise. He knew full well that his older colleague and sometime mentor was not impressed by rank. But this was the first time in Vledder's memory that DeKok had made a direct allusion to his contempt for rank. Vledder was well acquainted with DeKok's abhorrence of order and discipline. The often brilliant Detective-Inspector simply did not seem to fit in the rigid harness of official hierarchy. It was impossible to contain him with rules and regulations. The gray sleuth was too individualistic. It explained why he would never be promoted beyond his present rank and DeKok seemed happy with the arrangement. His seniority and brilliance, his obvious suitability for the important aspects of police work, guaranteed his continued employment and that was all he cared about.

---

* Commissaris: a rank equivalent to Captain. There are only two ranks higher: Chief-Commissaris and Chief Constable. Each jurisdiction has only a single Chief Constable, the highest possible police rank. There is one Chief Constable for all of Amsterdam. Other ranks in the Municipal Police are: Constable, Constable First Class, Sergeant, Adjutant, Inspector, Chief-Inspector and Commissaris. Adjutants and below are equivalent to non-commissioned ranks. Inspector is a rank equivalent to 2nd Lieutenant.

Constable Albert Cornelis, one of the newer additions to the force, entered the detective room and let his eyes roam through the area until he discovered DeKok. With long steps he approached the gray sleuth and handed him a yellow envelope.

"For you," he said simply.

"But hasn't the mail been already?" asked DeKok.

"Sure," answered Albert, "but this is a special delivery. A little boy handed it in at the desk downstairs."

"Just like that?"

"What do you mean?"

"Didn't he say anything?"

"No, the kid put the envelope on the desk and walked out again."

"What sort of boy?"

The constable shrugged his shoulders.

"I don't know. About eight. One of the little criminals from the neighborhood, I think."

"You know him?"

"No," grimaced the young constable. "As far as I know I've never seen him before."

"In that case," said DeKok, a hard gleam in his eyes, "I thank you to keep your snap judgements to yourself in future. I particularly dislike hearing an eight-year-old referred to as 'a little criminal' without any further evidence other than your prejudiced, ill-informed, unwanted and probably inaccurate opinion."

The young constable lost some color on his face and came to attention.

"Thank you," said DeKok mildly and waved him away.

Constable Cornelis made an about-face and marched out of the room. He would have something to add to the ever-growing store of anecdotes about DeKok. He had only been assigned to Warmoes Street in the last two months, straight from the Police

Academy. From time to time he had seen DeKok, an old, ineffective plainclothes man, he had thought, dressed in a rumpled raincoat and a ridiculous little felt hat that he usually wore far back on his head. The man seemed to waddle in and out of the station at all hours and the Commissaris did not like him. He had not, until now, understood the awe with which some people spoke about the old veteran. Surely, he had thought, the stories he had heard did not apply to this unprepossessing figure? He was a lot less sure of that after his brush with the steel in DeKok's eyes.

With an amused smile on his face, Vledder watched the constable leave. Usually DeKok was one of the most amicable, relaxed and humane people he knew. But then, unexpectedly, something would rub him the wrong way and he most resembled a bear suddenly wakened from deep hibernation. DeKok's craggy face, with the good-natured expression of an aged boxer, would be transformed into an expressionless mask and he could say the most biting things. At times, thankfully not often, Vledder had seen his old partner display all the symptoms of a beserker rage. DeKok was a complex person, too complicated for his own good, thought Vledder, unaware that this was sometimes exactly DeKok's own opinion of himself.

Vledder returned his attention to his partner on the desk next to his.

DeKok studied the envelope intently. *Personal*, it said at the top and underneath was written: *DeKok, detective, Warmoes Street station, Amsterdam*. That was all. There was no name, or address, of a sender. There was no stamp and no post-mark. Apparently the letter had been intended to be mailed, otherwise why add "Amsterdam"? The edges of the envelope were smudged and wrinkled. The letter must have been carried around for some time, in a purse, or pocket. DeKok brought the envelope closer to his face and sniffed. The sweet smell of some perfume teased his nose. He pushed himself further back, took his legs off the desk and used the tip of a pencil to open the envelope. He did it hastily, but carefully. Suddenly he had the indeterminate feeling that something important was contained in the envelope. Much to his surprise, the contents consisted of a death announcement with a purple border.

Vledder came to stand next to his desk.

"Who's dead?" he asked, interested.

DeKok unfolded the announcement.

"It has been the will of the Lord," he read, "to take from us, after a brief suffering, my dear husband and caring father Frederik Johannes Dinterloo at the age of thirty-two years."

DeKok shook his head sadly.

"So young," he regretted.

"But who is this Dinterloo?" asked Vledder impatiently, "And why do we get a copy of his death announcement?"

DeKok did not answer.

"The body will be committed to the grave," he read on, "on Thursday, the twenty-seventh next, at eleven of the clock in the morning at Sorrow Fields on the Amstel in Amsterdam. *Deo Volente*. At the request of the deceased: no crocuses, or other flowers."

"Who's Dinterloo?" asked Vledder again, more impatiently.

"I don't know," said DeKok. "I've never heard of him. Most certainly *not* somebody we've encountered in a professional capacity."

He looked at the backside of the announcement. With surprise he discovered in one corner a vague, almost illegible scribble in pencil. He leaned forward, held the paper against the light, moved it closer and than further away. Suddenly he could read the small, scribbly, but recognizable letters: *If you want to meet the next victim, you're cordially invited to attend the funeral.*

He studied the scribbles carefully and then handed the announcement to Vledder.

"Look in the lower left-hand corner," he advised.

Vledder took the piece of paper and did as he was asked. His eyes widened when he absorbed the portent of the message.

"The *next* victim," he said, obviously perplexed.

DeKok looked at the calendar on the wall.

"Isn't today Thursday?" he asked.

"The twenty-seventh," confirmed Vledder.

The old sleuth consulted his watch. Slowly he rose.

"It's nearly ten thirty," he said. "If we hurry, Deo volente, we'll be on time."

"What's this Deo volente business?" asked Vledder. "What does it mean?"

"If God wills," said DeKok and grabbed his hat.

* * *

Sorrow Fields was a busy place. Cars were parked bumper to bumper and Dick Vledder managed to park the old police VW with some difficulty between a light-blue Cadillac and a cream-colored Jaguar.

"Expensive funeral," he grinned. "A little farther down I saw a Rolls Royce."

"The car with the chauffeur?" asked DeKok, who knew little about cars and cared less. A car was a form of transportation, as far as he was concerned. His least favorite form of transportation and the fact that they came in all kinds of models and colors was something he blissfully ignored. Some were bigger than others and if it was big and square it was probably a Rolls Royce. Or not, he thought unconcernedly.

12

They left their old VW and walked across the gravel of the driveway. A group of people with blank faces waited in front of the Chapel. When the doors opened they went inside. The two Inspectors found a place in the back and leaned against the wall. Heavy organ music descended from the rafters and seemed to envelop the audience in a layer of sound. When the last tones died away, a small man, dressed in black, approached the rostrum.

He took a piece of paper from a pocket and spoke glibly about the inconsolable grief of the survivors. Then he touched upon the great service the deceased had performed for an organization to which he had "been devoted with heart and soul".

DeKok listened for a grain of sincerity, but the words were mechanical, obligatory, without inspiration or feeling. He allowed his gaze to wander over the audience and wondered who, among those present, had sent him the death announcement. What was that man's, or woman's, purpose? Was the dead Dinterloo indeed a victim, as the mention of a "next" victim seemed to imply? If so, of what? Or whom?

New organ sounds spewed forth. The man had left the rostrum, taking his papers with him. For the next performance, thought DeKok. Every time he attended a funeral, he was again struck by the Dutch habit of using a non-denominational Chapel for all funeral services. Since the Chapel was right on the funeral grounds it made for efficiency, there was no denying that. On a "good" day, depending on the size of the various groups and the number of rooms available, a funeral could be "processed" about every ten minutes, or so. For a moment DeKok was staggered by the numbers. That was about six corpses an hour, say ten hours a day, including weekends, of course. Multiply that by the number of cemeteries in Amsterdam and the result was more than three thousand funerals a week. Thankfully he realized that only a very small percentage of all those deaths came under his jurisdiction.

A group of professional pallbearers came in and arranged themselves around the coffin. Wide doors opened behind them and cheerful sunlight danced inside. The pallbearers lifted the coffin and carried it away into the light. The audience rose and shuffled into some sort of order. DeKok looked back. The front doors were already opened for the next group.

Outside they followed the coffin and the mourners. They kept a little distance between themselves and the last of the group. It was warm and the walk to the grave-site was long. Vledder glanced at DeKok.

"Any sign of the next victim?" he asked. "With the exception of the funeral personnel, I counted fifty-seven people." He gestured at the group ahead. "It should be one of those." He fell silent, chewed his lower lip. "Unless," he added, "somebody is acting out a stupid joke."

The group tightened up, the stragglers hastened to catch up as the visitors arranged themselves in a loose circle around the grave. DeKok paid no attention to the coffin. He studied the crowd, hoping for a sign, a gesture, some indication from the person who had directed him here. Who?

The pallbearers took away the black cloth that covered the coffin and placed the now bare coffin on the grave lift. A bird sang in the distance and the wind hushed through the tree tops. A young woman cried soundlessly, worried a handkerchief in her hands. DeKok pulled his lower lip and let it plop back. Several people turned around to look for the origin of the disgusting sound. DeKok looked at them and stored the information away. Vledder had counted fifty-seven people. About two thirds of them were men. Ages seemed to range from about mid-twenties to early sixties. The women all looked beautiful . . . even the older ones.

The young woman who had been crying received a small shovel from one of the funeral people. With uncontrolled movements she shoveled some earth on the coffin. She was the only person who showed any emotion at all ... a barely controlled expression of real sorrow. The others all seemed to perform some obscure rite, unemotional, solemn, like a farmer on his way to church.

The circle broke up. Slowly the visitors went their various ways. The young woman was ahead of the others. Next to her was an older woman, who supported her by an elbow. Then followed the graying gentlemen. DeKok recognized them from their attitudes, their looks, their eyes ... company executives, captains of industry, the nobility of these modern times. The old sleuth wondered to which particular clan they belonged, why they had lent themselves to appear at this funeral.

After a few minutes, the two cops walked down a side path. The younger man kicked the gravel and cursed under his breath.

"What a stupid joke with that Announcement," he hissed between his teeth. "I wish I had whoever did it in my hands, right now. We certainly have better things to do than waste our time in cemeteries."

DeKok did not react. At times he could ignore anything, or anybody, with sublime indifference. This habit had brought some people to the edge of despair. Meanwhile his gaze followed the group on the parallel path to theirs. If it was true, he thought, that a victim had just been buried and that the next victim was among those who had attended the funeral, the murderer could not be far way. He pressed his lips together and grinned to himself. Murderer ... who said anything about a murder?

He glanced at Vledder.

"When we get back to the office," he suggested, "why don't you look up the Death Certificate?"

"You mean the official cause of death for Dinterloo?" There was surprise in Vledder's voice.

"Exactly," agreed DeKok, unperturbed. "And try to find out some more about him . . . work, family, male friends, female friends, that sort of thing."

Vledder looked at him, a disbelieving smile on his face.

"You're taking this serious?"

DeKok made a nonchalant gesture.

"Unless . . . unless you've some imperative objections?" There was just a hint of mockery in his tone.

"It's just silly," snorted Vledder, visibly irritated. "Just plain silly. Some kind of joker sends you a death announcement with some barely legible scribbles and you run with it."

DeKok smiled broadly.

"Run with it," he said with delight. "That's it . . . run with it." He adjusted his collar and took another path, away from the group he had been observing. As soon as they could no longer see him, as soon as he was hidden by some greenery, he started to run. His collar was loose and his coat and tie fluttered after him. He held his hat in one hand as he moved at a surprising speed. Vledder watched him go, amused. DeKok at speed was a comical sight.

Vledder started to move as well. It took only a short sprint for the young, athletic man to pace his partner.

"What are you doing?" he asked.

"I want to be at the exit before the others," panted DeKok.

"Why?"

"The license tags . . . I want the license tags of all the cars of all the people in that group."

Vledder nodded his understanding.

Via a maze of little lanes, paths and bridges, they reached the exit. From a distance they saw the mourners take formal leave of each other in front of the Chapel.

Quickly the two men walked down the rows of cars and wrote down the license tags. Later they could cross off those they did not need, or want. Another peculiarity, thought DeKok. A wise City Council had decreed that only official funeral vehicles could enter the terrain of a cemetery and all traffic from the Chapel to the grave-site was on foot. In America, so he had heard, people would simply refuse to die if they could not go to their grave by car. He had heard, but relegated it to the realm of obscene fiction, that in the United States they even had drive-through funeral parlors, where the deceased was displayed in a window, like an macabre antique. Be that as it may, he thought, right now the Amsterdam ordinance makes it a lot easier to get the necessary license numbers.

The driver of the Rolls Royce was seated on the running board of the expensive car, reading a newspaper. As the Inspectors passed, he gave them a friendly nod.

DeKok stopped and pointed at the car.

"Is it real?" he asked, showing a stupid eagerness that belied his total disinterest in the subject of cars.

"You mean . . . a Rolls Royce?" asked the driver, smiling.

"The dream of my youth," lied DeKok.

The driver looked at him.

"You should be glad," he sighed, "that you didn't realize your dream."

DeKok looked at the driver. He liked the open, honest face with narrow creases around the eyes and the hint of a ready smile around the mouth.

"I . . . eh, I don't understand."

The man looked sad.

"You have to do all sorts of things to get a car like this," he said. "And then you have to do more things in order to *keep* it. Perhaps that's the most difficult thing to do." It sounded philosophical, didactic. "And in this life it doesn't just apply to beautiful cars either," he added. He straightened out his cap and took a deep breath. "You see, sir, if you . . ."

17

Suddenly he stopped and put away his newspaper. His eyes moved past DeKok into the distance. The old Inspector turned around and followed his gaze. A part of the group was leaving the cemetery. In front walked a big man with dark, horn-rimmed glasses. DeKok thought he recognized the man. He groped among his memories as he watched the man approach. He had seen him somewhere, had spoken to him.

For just another second or so he waited, then he took Vledder by the arm and steered him in the direction of the old police VW. The younger man produced the keys and unlocked the doors. DeKok struggled into the passenger seat. Suddenly he noticed a card under the left wiper. He nudged Vledder and pointed at it. The young man stepped out of the car, took the card from the windshield and gave it to his partner.

It was pink and smelled of perfume.

"Come to Casa Erotica," he read out loud, "the new sex theater at Rear Fort Canal."

He turned the card in his hand and suddenly became alert. The same, scribbly, small letters were on the back of the card.

"*Ask for the Naked Lady.*" it said.

"What's the matter?" asked Vledder, who had seen DeKok stiffen.

DeKok swallowed.

"The Naked Lady," he said hoarsely.

2

Vledder cleared his throat.

"Professor Doctor Frederik Johannes Dinterloo," he said formally.

DeKok was surprised.

"What!?" he exclaimed incredulously. "Dinterloo was a *professor*?"

His young partner laughed at the reaction.

"Indeed . . . until a year and a half ago he held the highest academic rank at the Technical University of Twente, in Enschede."

DeKok's eyebrows rippled with that startling movement that surprised people so often. At times it seemed that DeKok's eyebrows lived a life of their own. Vledder had never been able to muster the temerity to ask DeKok to repeat the phenomenon on request and by now he was convinced that it was a totally involuntary movement. DeKok never seemed to be aware of it.

"But he was only thirty-two years old when he died," objected DeKok. "As I remember, in order to become a *professor*, you must first obtain a doctorate and then it still takes years and years."

Vledder waited for the display on DeKok's forehead to subside. He was not about to interrupt the remarkable eyebrow gymnastics with mere words. When DeKok's forehead again had come to rest, Vledder answered.

"You're right," he said. "Dinterloo was one of Holland's youngest professors. An extremely gifted young man. He was barely twenty-eight when he was unanimously selected by the College of Professors. At the time it caused a lot of publicity. About a year and half ago he was lured away by ITO, International Tropic Oil."

"What do you mean, *lured* away?"

Vledder sighed.

"They offered him a mansion, a fantastic salary, his own laboratory and complete freedom of research."

"Tempting."

Vledder gestured.

"Of course it was tempting. Especially the freedom to do independent research was an important point. Dinterloo was, after all, more the researcher type than the teacher type. He was extremely inventive and productive."

DeKok looked at his partner with admiration.

"You're well informed," he said warmly. "And in such a short time."

Vledder blushed at the praise.

"That's what computers are for," he began. "As soon as I knew the name, I hooked up to . . ."

"Spare me the details," growled DeKok. "I know you can make that machine read and write. But I want human information, not statistics."

Vledder grinned. He was not offended. DeKok had never used the computer terminal on his desk, probably did not even know the location of the power switch.

"Well," said the young man, "you're in luck. A cousin of mine studied in Twente. As soon as I knew that Dinterloo used to teach there, I called him. As it happened, my cousin knew him well, attended a number of his courses."

"How was the relationship with his students?"

"Not so good." Vledder slowly shook his head. "Dinterloo was rather stiff, reserved, self-contained. He had few social contacts. In fact, he was only interested in his work, which was also his hobby: science. Everything else, politics, human interactions, social events . . . they didn't interest him. He didn't understand them. Sometimes that caused trouble, especially in the academic world, which is as political as any."

"An extra inducement to accept the offer from International Tropic Oil." DeKok rubbed his chin thoughtfully.

"I think so," agreed Vledder.

"And all those expensive cars at the cemetery? ITO big-whigs?"

"Yes," nodded Vledder, "Directors, Presidents, Vice Presidents, Managers, you name it . . . the top brass."

"And the less expensive cars?"

Vledder's fingers flew over his keyboard and figures appeared on the screen. DeKok was glad to notice that his young friend seemed to compare the information on the screen with the scribbles in his notebook, the true policeman's inseparable companion.

"Some of the cars were not connected," said Vledder. "You will remember that we wrote down numbers rather indiscriminately. But after sorting through it all, the less expensive cars belonged mostly to the Dinterloo family members and some secretaries. Let's see . . . two VWs . . . the father and a younger brother, a Fiat 850 belonging to an unmarried sister, a Ford registered in the name of a brother-in-law." He grinned. "There was even an old 2CV, an "Ugly Duckling", belonging to a former student."

"All the way from Twente?"

"Yes. Lilian Hernandez."

"Love?"

"A relationship with the victim?"

"Exactly," said DeKok, reflecting that Hernandez was a perfectly good Dutch name. Ever since the Spanish and Portuguese Jews had fled to Holland, sometime in the 15th Century, Hispanic names had been commonplace. Later the Huguenots had fled from an ever increasingly oppressive France to come to Holland, adding French names. Through the ages Holland had been a haven of tolerance in a world filled with prejudice and persecution. Comparatively speaking of course, added DeKok to himself. Anyway, he thought cynically, intolerance was just plain bad for business. His eclectic mind had no trouble associating 15th Century Jews, the Dutch East India Company and International Tropic Oil with the apparent mystery of the late Professor Dinterloo.

Meanwhile he listened to his partner.

"How would I know?" protested Vledder, spreading wide his arms. "He has been married for seven years. Happily married by all accounts. We saw his wife at the funeral, with her mother. There's also a three-year old daughter."

DeKok looked somber.

"*My dear husband and caring father,*" he recited sadly. He looked at Vledder. "What was the cause of death?"

"There's no Death Certificate as such. No 'cause of death' ... but the result of an inquest."

DeKok sat up straight.

"Inquest? Dinterloo died a violent death?"

"Yes. He drowned."

"He drowned?" swallowed DeKok.

"Yes," nodded Vledder. "Just a normal drowning. Here's the report of the inquest." He handed the copy to DeKok. "On a dark night Dinterloo drove into the North-Holland Canal and drowned."

"Where?"

"Near Ilpendam. Just past the soccer field. He came from the north and was apparently on his way home."

"Alcohol?"

Vledder made a helpless gesture.

"There was no autopsy. The local Judge-Advocate didn't think it necessary. It was generally assumed that oncoming traffic blinded him and caused him to lose control. There was a written declaration by some witnesses. A Mr. and Mrs. Wien who were driving a car behind Dinterloo. They saw the accident and immediately stopped and flagged down other cars. There was a lot of help. It's a rather busy road. But Dinterloo had already drowned before they could get him out of the car. Apparently he banged his head on the steering wheel which caused unconsciousness. There was subcutaneous bleeding on the forehead."

"He was alone in the car?"

"Presumably. No other victims were found. It is of course possible that a passenger survived the accident and refuses to come forward, for whatever reason."

DeKok looked skeptical.

"With that many witnesses on the scene?"

Vledder shrugged his shoulders.

"The door on the passenger side wasn't locked."

DeKok shook his head.

"Doesn't necessarily mean anything." He rubbed the bridge of his nose with a little finger. Then he held the finger in the air as if he had never seen it before. After some contemplation he asked reluctantly: "What about the car?"

"An Opel Rekord. Almost new, less than ten thousand miles." The reason for DeKok's reluctance soon became clear as

25

Vledder started to add the more technical details. "Mechanically in excellent condition," continued the young man. "No severed brake lines, no weakened steering mechanism, no transmission problems, electrical systems all in A-1 condition, tires . . ."

DeKok, who had only a vague idea what Vledder was talking about, held up a hand in protest and rose from his chair. He paced a few times up and down the large room and then stopped in front of Vledder's desk.

"How was Dinterloo's health? Did he wear glasses?"

Vledder sat up straight, an irritated look in his eyes. His face was getting red.

"What *are* you after?" he exclaimed. "There's nothing mysterious about Dinterloo's death. Maybe a few drinks, driving too fast . . . drowned. Every year thousands die the same way. It was just an accident. In God's name, what else can it be?"

The gray sleuth looked at him for a long time.

"You know," he said softly, "a lot of murders have been committed in God's name."

Without another word he turned around and walked over to the coat rack and grabbed his ridiculous little hat.

"Where are you going?" asked Vledder.

DeKok grinned mischievously.

"To Casa Erotica. I want to see what a Naked Lady looks like."

* * *

They left the station house and walked deeper into the Red Light District. As usual, it was busy. Clusters of people pushed against each other in front of the windows of the sex-shops. Men spoke loudly and excitedly in many languages. Women laughed, giggled, or bargained for prices as they offered their services. A drunk, there was always a drunk, bumped his way through the crowds.

At the end of the street they turned right toward Rear Fort Canal. Neon lights in many colors framed the doors to the various sex-theaters. Those whores who did not have their own window, could be found here. On the darker stretches of the canal they hissed a menu of their services at the passers-by. Their demeanor changed when they saw DeKok. Most of them just smiled at the gray man, but some would call out a cheery greeting. With the exception of an occasional teasing remark, they ignored Vledder. In general DeKok greeted back politely and a few times he lifted his hat a few centimeters above his head. Vledder did not react in any way.

In front of *Casa Erotica*, DeKok stopped and planted himself in front of the facade.

"Live show," he read aloud. He looked at Vledder with a twinkling in his eyes. "I don't know if I should take you inside," he teased. "What will Celine say?"

"My fiancee isn't all that puritan," growled Vledder. "Besides, I'm on duty."

"You're right," agreed DeKok. "You're on duty."

He stepped over to the cashier and asked for Frisian Ben. The man pointed vaguely toward the back and yelled something. A large, heavily-built man with a frivolous purple shirt came through the swinging doors. A happy look of recognition lit up his pale, hazel eyes.

"Well, well, well, DeKok," he called jovially. "You've finally come to visit me."

"No," denied DeKok, "I'm here for the 'Naked Lady'."

Frisian Ben laughed uproariously.

"Naked lady? Which one? Naked ... they're all naked. Naked as the day they were born. It's their business, you see. They make a living that way ... and me." Grinning, he waved toward the dark entrance behind the swing doors. "Come in. We'll start in a few minutes. I've got a new act . . . *very* realistic."

DeKok made a restraining gesture.

"I'm not here for the show." He looked the operator in the face, a meaningful look in his eyes. "I'm here for the 'Naked Lady'."

Frisian Ben laughed again. For a moment Vledder suspected he would slap himself on the knee.

"That's what you said . . . naked lady."

DeKok remained serious.

"That's what I said," he repeated with some emphasis, ". . . 'Naked Lady'."

The laughter disappeared from the face of the large Frisian. He looked searchingly at DeKok. He finally realized that there was something behind DeKok's question, something serious.

"Are you looking for one of them?" he asked suspiciously. "Do you want one of them?"

"Perhaps."

The big man raised his hands in a gesture of despair.

"Just tell me who. I've got seven of them. All *nice* girls, as far as I know . . . straight from their mother, practically virgins."

"That," grinned DeKok, "I find hard to believe."

Ben looked insulted.

"I mean, as a matter of speaking. I only have respectable girls in my show. No business girls, you understand, no *tomijers*.* I even have some college girls."

"Oh yes," interrupted Vledder, "what do they study? Sociology?"

Ben gave him a denigrating look, then turned back to DeKok.

---

* *tomijer* = Amsterdam underworld slang for prostitute.

"What do you want from me?" he exclaimed "Of course I don't operate a finishing school for young ladies."

DeKok placed a friendly hand on the man's shoulder.

"Don't get excited," he said soothingly. "Do you have a moment? I want to talk."

Frisian Ben sighed elaborately.

"All right," he said resignedly. "All right, let's go to my office."

He pushed open a side door and led the way up a narrow wooden stair. The second floor was large, roomy with heavy oak beams supporting the floor above. Ben turned around.

"It was an old warehouse," he said proudly, "I had it remodelled."

The decor was bizarre and tasteless with a large bar in the center, surrounded by barstools of an undeterminate color and a lot of chrome. Along the sides were wide sofas and large easy chairs. On the walls were life-size portraits of beautiful nude women in obscene poses. Attractive and vulgar. Spotlights were situated between the beams, aimed at a glass stage.

Frisian Ben waved expansively.

"Take the load off your feet," he invited. "Take it easy and tell me what I can do for you."

DeKok did not respond at once. Thoughtfully he chewed his lower lip while he seemed absorbed in one of the pictures on the wall. The picture was of a beautiful young girl with a gamin face who stared at the room from between her legs. A small light over the picture insured that not a detail was lost on the viewer. But DeKok did not see it. In his mind he searched for an opening to the conversation. His direct question about a "Naked Lady" had not resulted in a satisfactory answer. The proprietor of *Casa Erotica* had not understood him, or had not wanted to understand him. On the whole he felt that Ben's response had been candid. "Naked Lady" did not mean a thing to him, certainly no more than the seven naked graces he already had under contract. DeKok's eyes came back into focus and he pointed at the stage.

"Floor show?"

"Yes."

"Like downstairs?"

"Downstairs," grinned Ben, "is for the general public."

"And here?"

The sex-exploiter plucked at his purple shirt.

"The rich guys want something too . . . they want to see things, experience things."

"Closed meetings, private parties," understood DeKok.

The big man nodded, ill at ease.

"Like for . . . ITO . . . Tropic Oil?"

Ben looked at him, an alert look in his eyes.

"I . . . I'd be a bad businessman," he said carefully, "if I revealed the names of my clients."

DeKok pressed his lips together. His friendly expression disappeared.

"I don't work for a scandal sheet," he said sharply. "I don't care one whit about what the gentlemen do when they're here. I don't even care who they are, government people, foreigners, whatever. It's all the same to me. But I *do* want to know if the people from Tropic Oil visit here."

"Why?"

DeKok made a theatrical gesture.

"Because," he said slowly, "I need the information for an ongoing investigation." He paused, then added: "And it's no use to ask what sort of investigation, because I'm not at liberty to reveal that at this time."

"All right," admitted Frisian Ben reluctantly, "they come here from time to time."

"How many?"

"A dozen, fifteen, sometimes more."

"When was the last time?"

"About a week ago."

"Do you know them?"

"You mean by name?"

"Yes."

"Of course not." He shook his head. "Usually I get a phone call from some secretary. We agree on a certain evening and afterwards I get a check. That's all. Other than that I have no contact with the gentlemen."

"What about the girls?"

"If the kids want to make some extra money . . . who am I to stand in their way. After all . . ." Suddenly he stopped and looked intently at DeKok. His face became serious and there was no hint of hilarity when he asked: "Is it about Sylvie?"

"Why Sylvie?" asked DeKok, evading the question.

"Sylvie," swallowed Ben, "disappeared that night . . . the night of Tropic Oil."

3

Inspector DeKok leaned his elbows on the desk and shook his gray head with irritation.

"Stupid people," he hissed between his teeth. "Accomplished business men, sharp, opportunistic, clever, but when lust tickles their slow-moving blood they turn into school boys, stupid, besotted and helpless. They endanger their own and other's happiness, risk disease and disgrace and . . ." He did not complete the sentence. "For crying out loud," he said in an exasperated tone of voice, "all those girls at Casa Erotica have their names and private numbers in notebooks. They even exchange information among each other."

Vledder grinned boyishly.

"I thought the pictures rather amusing," he said. "Those guys actually sent inscribed photographs of themselves to their lady loves."

"*With love from your Teddy Bear*," recited DeKok sadly. "Nice for later. Blackmail as dessert . . . why not?"

"What does it matter?" smiled Vledder. "Why bother about it? I, for one, am happy those guys were so stupid. It certainly made our work a lot easier."

With a satisfied look on his face he arranged his notes in a neat pile and at the same time, almost casually, fired up his computer terminal. Soon images and other information started to flash across the screen as he methodically turned each piece of paper and every pertinent page of his notebook.

"To summarize," Vledder said finally, "on what I call the 'Tropic Oil Night', there was a very private party upstairs at Casa Erotica at Rear Fort Canal . . . the party was more wild than usual and the entertainment was more abandoned than usual . . . the booze flowed copiously and all the gentlemen we saw at the funeral were eager participants in the festivities."

"Including the man in the coffin," added DeKok grimly.

"And he was *very* drunk," agreed Vledder. "According to the girls, Dinterloo was one of the regulars at these orgies and became drunk with the regularity of a clock."

DeKok held a finger up in the air.

"This time, however, he was so drunk that he addressed the esteemed Chairman of Tropic Oil after he had gained his undivided attention by throwing a tumbler of whiskey in his face." The gray sleuth grinned evilly. "Mister Gellecom," he mimicked with a thick tongue, "thou art a viper."

"Not a viper." Vledder shook his head. "He called him a cobra."

DeKok laughed heartily.

"A very apt description, if you ask me. I also remember him from the funeral. He was the man with the Rolls Royce, the car with the driver," he added hastily, just in case he had identified the wrong type of car. He paused briefly. "At the time he looked familiar and now I remember I saw him on TV at one time or another. Some talk-show. A well-preserved fifty or so, slow movements and an alert, suspicious look in his eyes." He shook his head. "Not the type of man who can take a joke."

"What do you mean?"

"Exactly what I'm saying. Gellecom isn't the sort of man who will gladly suffer a tumbler full of whiskey in his face.

Sylvie must have realized that at once. I'm sure she analyzed the look in the man's eyes correctly. Those girls could teach a psychologist a trick or two, you know." Vledder guffawed at the unintentional pun. DeKok continued unperturbed: "It's a good thing she took care of Dinterloo and led him out of harm's way."

"But nobody has seen hide or hair of her since then," objected Vledder. He looked at his partner. "What do you think? Could she be the 'Naked Lady'?"

DeKok shrugged.

"Based on what we know so far, it's certainly possible. But who exactly is the 'Naked Lady'? There's just no sense to it, the Quarter is full of naked ladies as Ben so abundantly made clear. But," he added briskly, "I suggest we find the girl as soon as possible."

"Why?"

"I want to know her whereabouts," sighed DeKok. "I want to know she's all right."

"Surely you don't think something has happened to her? What would be the sense of *that*?"

DeKok pushed his lower lip forward. There was a stubborn look on his face.

"Maybe she knows what happened to Dinterloo that night."

"The night of the orgy?" Vledder was surprised.

"Yes."

"Nothing happened that night," mocked Vledder. "He didn't hit the water until two days later."

DeKok nodded to himself. For all Vledder knew, he had not even been heard.

"What do we know about her?" asked DeKok.

Reluctantly, Vledder consulted his notes.

"Sylvie Rebergen," he read out loud. "Twenty-three years old. She ran away from home for the first time when she was sixteen. She was apprehended several times and returned to parental care. Despite extensive help from Social Services and the Juvenile Protection People, she continually ran away from home. She married at the age of eighteen, one Jacob Vantong, an elderly, comfortable business man and she's currently still involved in divorce proceedings. She's been stripping since she was nineteen. According to experts, she enjoys her work. She has numerous relationships with men and is discreetly known as an expensive call-girl who, according to some of her clients, is worth every penny." He looked up. "Not exactly a girl who's in danger of *succumbing to physical and psychological turpitude*."* He paused, grinned and added: "I'd say that she is a danger to the physical and psychological turpitude of *others*."

"But she disappeared," said DeKok curtly.

Vledder made an impatient gesture.

"Sure. It's a coincidence. I agree. But that doesn't mean there's any connection between her disappearance and Dinterloo's death. For all we know she's somewhere in the Mediterranean with the boy-friend of the hour."

"Possibly." DeKok pursed his lips. Then he looked at Vledder. "Do you have her address?" he asked.

"Sure. 984 Fleder Court. An apartment in the suburbs."

* * *

It was a nice summer day. A friendly sun was high in the sky and stately cumulus clouds floated against a stark blue background. A soft, cool breeze banished oppressive heat without causing a chill.

Vledder and DeKok had reached the ninth floor of the huge apartment building that rose from the surrounding meadows and fields. As is usual in Holland, a long gallery runs along the

---

* Police expression: used as motivation to return under-age persons to the supervision of parents or guardians. The age of consent in the Netherlands is 21 years.

outside of each floor and the front doors of the apartments open up to the balcony on the outside of the building. The galleries become streets with elevators and stairs at either end of the long buildings. For some inexplicable reason, despite the often inclement weather, few apartment buildings have entrances on the inside.

DeKok ignored the magnificent view, pushed his little hat firmer down on his gray hair and studied the numbering. Then he walked in the direction of 984. He stopped in front of the door and studied the discreet name plate next to the doorbell. *sylvie rebergen* it announced in small black script without capital letters.

Vledder pushed the bell and waited. Several minutes went by without a sound from inside. Vledder again pushed the bell.

DeKok went over to the windows and tried to look inside. The windows were covered from the inside by venetian blinds and thick, heavy curtains. The interior remained a mystery.

After some time DeKok produced a small brass cylinder, a gift from a former burglar, his friend Handy Henkie. The clever little contraption had allowed all doors to be opened for DeKok. This time, too, he had little problem with the uncomplicated lock.

"Breaking and entering," chided Vledder, who no longer protested when DeKok used this unorthodox method to gain entry.

"Oh, well," shrugged DeKok without a sign of remorse and pushed open the door.

From a small foyer they entered a roomy hall. The light was diffused and came from a smoked glass panel off to one side. There was an oak coat rack and two fashionable ladies coats hung from the pegs. Next to the coat rack was an old-fashioned chest, once used to store blankets. The chest was intricately carved in a design that matched the carvings on the coat rack.

DeKok lifted the lid. The chest was empty. Slowly he replaced the lid. The hinges screeched.

There was an unidentifiable, threatening atmosphere in the apartment ... a tense, oppressive feeling that was palpable. DeKok felt the tension in the tips of his fingers. Vledder's breathing was shallow and labored. DeKok sniffed like a bloodhound on a familiar spoor. He had recognized the faint scent of perfume.

A door was ajar to the right of the hallway. DeKok approached the door thoughtfully and pushed it wider with the tip of his shoe. Slowly the door opened wider. A part of the room became visible. The beautiful body of a young woman rested on a white woollen blanket, intimately illuminated by the light of a pink lamp.

Vledder looked over DeKok's shoulder.

"Sylvie," he panted.

DeKok nodded soberly.

"Murdered."

* * *

A hard look came in DeKok's eyes. His face became a mask. During his long career he had seen many murder victims, but seldom had death presented itself as abhorrent as this time. It had a dazing effect, as if he was drugged. With an effort he shook off the lethargic feeling, entered the room and leaned over the corpse. She was on her right side, the lower legs elegantly crossed at the slender ankles. A thin stream of coagulated blood trailed down from the mutilated eye sockets. It had formed a small puddle on the white blanket.

He felt her cheek, but there was no doubt. She was dead. The chill of her skin seemed to suck the warmth from his hand. It was an eery feeling.

He straightened up and looked around the room. Nearby, on a glass table were some pink cards. Nicely printed, expensive cards.

"Come to Casa Erotica," he read out loud, "the new sex theater at Rear Fort Canal."

Absent-mindedly he rifled the cards through his hands. Suddenly he noticed a blemish on the back of one of the cards. He looked closer and discovered some writing on the back of one of the cards. He held it up to the lights. He saw small, scribbly, but very legible letters: *Fred Dinterloo, 387 Rose Lane, Bloemendaal.*

4

The gray sleuth waved defensively. A sarcastic smile curled the corners of his mouth.

"No, definitely not," he said mildly but with determination. "I don't feel like getting involved in an investigation that has been going on for months."

Commissaris Buitendam, the tall, stately chief of Warmoes Street station, gestured violently. His normal demeanor was that of a diplomat from an earlier century. As he came closer to his pension, thought DeKok, he also seems to get more pompous. He watched with interest as red spots appeared on the commissarial cheeks.

"DeKok," said the Commissaris excitedly, "I don't want to give a man like you specific orders." His tone was both belligerent and aristocratic, but with an undertone of conciliation. He was obviously trying to control himself, but there was a hint of a threat in his voice all the same. "But, especially in connection with the death of . . ." He paused, looked at some notes. ". . . Sylvie Rebergen . . ." He paused again. This time because DeKok was shaking his head.

"It was no more than coincidence," said DeKok. "I wasn't looking for a maniac . . . nothing was further from my mind. I was looking into the background of the young professor."

Buitendam pressed his thin lips together. He glared at his subordinate.

"Now that a victim has been found in *our* jurisdiction," continued the Chief, "I want you to be in charge of the investigations. We should handle the case."

"All of it?" asked DeKok, confused.

"Yes, indeed," confirmed the Commissaris calmly. "This comes directly from the Chief Constable. He's of the opinion that modern methods have failed in this case."

"Well," answered DeKok, rubbing his gray hair, "I'd rather not. I know nothing about the case. I've not been involved. I know no more than what's been written up in the papers."

"That's a lame excuse," refuted his boss. "You simply cannot refuse, DeKok . . . it would be . . . eh, . . . indecent."

DeKok reacted obstreperously.

"It's downright indecent to lay such a task on the shoulders of an old man."

For a moment the Commissaris looked at him with open mouth. Few people knew that he and DeKok had attended the Police Academy together. They were almost of an age. The Commissaris shook his head as if to clear it.

"You can't use your age as an excuse," he reprimanded. "I've seen your latest fitness report and you're in excellent physical shape."

"Ah, well," sighed DeKok. "The carcass might still be functioning, but it's the mind, you see . . . it wanders." He shrugged apologetically, seemed to come to a decision. "All right," he said, more briskly, "let's have some details. How many victims have there been?"

The Commissaris quickly suppressed a sigh of relief.

"Eight," he said. "Eight, if we include Sylvie Rebergen . . . and in view of her injuries we should certainly include her. Yes, eight young women have been killed that way."

"And what has the special branch of Headquarters accomplished so far?"

The Commissaris bristled. For just a moment the chauvinism in favor of "his" own station was visible.

"Nothing," he exclaimed. "Not a thing ... as you know very well." He stepped from behind his desk and approached DeKok. His face was serious and he placed a hand on the shoulder of his best detective. "About half an hour ago they found the ninth victim of that maniac."

"Where?"

The Chief waved in the direction of the window.

"As I said, on *our* turf. On New Side Maelstrom, number forty-eight, second floor. I sent Kruger and Weelen ahead. They'll wait for you. The Chief Constable has left explicit instructions that *nothing* be done until you're on the scene."

"Nice of him," commented DeKok. He wiped a mocking smile off his face. "How much time do I have?"

"As long as you need, although ... we *would* like results as soon as possible."

"And I have a free hand?"

The Commissaris gave him a long, hard, considering look.

"Within the limits of the Law, DeKok." He looked with suspicion at the bland exterior of the man on the chair. "The Law, DeKok," he repeated with emphasis. "We fight in the name of the Law."

DeKok rose and walked toward the door.

"Sometimes," he said to himself, but the Commissaris was mercifully unable to hear him

* * *

With a gesture of suppressed anger Bram Weelen, the police photographer, tossed his beloved Hasselblad on a chair with such force that the expensive camera bounced several times.

"I'm going to be sick," he screamed. "I really am going to be sick this time. I am sick of looking into the crushed eyes of all these women. I'm going to throw up."

DeKok placed an arm around his shoulder.

"Take a deep breath," he advised. "Just take it easy for a while."

The photographer looked at him, breathing deeply.

"You know," said Bram softly, "that I have nightmares about it? Sometimes I wake up, drenched in sweat."

"Have you seen all of them?"

Bram Weelen pressed his lips together and swallowed as if keeping down his bile.

"Every time," he said in a subdued voice. "Either at the scene, or later, in the lab. I took the first few and now I've seen all nine. God knows how many more I'm going to get in my lens."

"Yes," answered DeKok, "God knows."

Bram Weelen did not respond. He seemed to recover somewhat and looked less upset. He glanced at DeKok.

"They really stuck it to you, this time, didn't they?" His tone was sympathetic.

"What do you mean?" asked the gray sleuth, surprise in his voice.

Weelen described a vague circle with his hand.

"To give you the case. It's a low trick, if you ask me. Do you know how long they have been trying to solve it?"

"About half a year."

"Right. And you know how many people have been assigned?"

"Not exactly." DeKok shook his head. "A few, I'd guess."

Weelen looked disgusted.

"A few is right," he commented bitterly. "A Chief-Inspector and his assistant, two Adjutants and about twenty sundry detectives. All under the overall supervision of a real-life Commissaris and with full assistance of all the technical support groups at Headquarters."

"Quite a chorus," smiled DeKok.

"Right," nodded Weelen vehemently, "a small army . . . and what have you got?"

DeKok turned half-way and pointed at the broad shoulders of a well-built young man who had squatted down next to the corpse and was busily writing in a notebook.

"I," he said with pride and affection in his voice, "I . . . have Dick Vledder. Together we've solved a few things here and there."

Weelen started to pack his equipment into his aluminum suitcase. When he was finished, he looked at the old cop.

"I wish you all the best, DeKok," he said sincerely.

He received a grateful nod in return.

"When will you have my pictures?"

"First thing in the morning."

DeKok nodded and waved him away. Meanwhile his gaze returned to the victim. She was on the floor in front of the sofa, supine on a luxurious carpet with a gay flowery pattern. She was dressed in a short, suede skirt and a tight-fitting black sweater. A scrap of a yellow scarf blazoned from under her chin. The arms were stretched out close to the body and the shapely legs were slightly spread. The fingers, crooked, claw-like, pointed at the ceiling.

He knelt next to her. Weelen had been right. The face was horribly mutilated. Both eyes had been pressed from the sockets like ripe grapes. From the corners of the sockets thin trails of coagulated blood had formed a puddle in the delicate ears. Dark red lumps of dried blood stuck to the blonde hair.

Because of the terrible damage to the eyes, it was difficult to guess her age. DeKok estimated it to be around twenty-five. The skin of the face was smooth and without a blemish, the mouth showed no sign of the network of fine wrinkles that inevitably appeared with older women.

Slowly he pushed himself upright and looked at the room. There was no mess, no disorder, no sign of a struggle.

Kruger, the fingerprint expert, appeared with a satisfied smile.

"The lady had a lot of visitors."

"How so?"

"So far," said Kruger, pointing with his badger-bristled brush, "I've found evidence of at least seven visitors."

"Where?"

"Almost everywhere. All over the house . . . in the kitchen, the bedroom and even in the shower." Kruger shook his head. "She wasn't a very clean housekeeper."

"Men?"

"Huh?"

"Do the prints belong to men?" asked DeKok patiently.

Kruger looked calculating.

"That's hard to say," he said finally. "I can't be one hundred percent certain . . . too many factors, you see." He looked at DeKok's face. "But," he added hastily, "at least four or five sets definitely belong to men."

"Identifiable?"

The dactyloscopist nodded enthusiastically.

"Oh, yes, excellent quality. If they are in our files, it will be no problem to get you a match."

DeKok scratched the tip of his nose. He remained silent for a long time. Finally he turned to Kruger.

"I take it you were involved with most of the others as well?" He pointed at the corpse.

"Oh, yes, almost all of them."

"Did they all look like that?"

"You mean the eyes?"

"Yes."

"Exactly the same. I didn't see the first two, but all the others were just like that. No difference. The only difference was the women. I mean, different types . . . smaller, bigger, fatter, younger, older. There was no line. The Headquarters guys could never discover a common thread."

"Strange."

Kruger did not answer. He leaned over his case and started to repack his large collection of brushes, bottles, jars, magnifying glasses and other paraphernalia.

"As soon as I have a match . . . if I have a match, you'll hear from me." Kruger moved toward the door. "Good luck," he wished in parting. He paused, looked at DeKok. "Believe me, you'll need it," he added. For just another moment he waited, hesitated, then he abruptly turned around and left.

"Luck," murmured DeKok under his breath, "is for the bold. Let's hope it applies in my case as well."

Dr. Koning, the old, eccentric Coroner was next. He stepped inside, followed by two morgue attendants and a stretcher. As usual, he was dressed in striped pants, an old-fashioned tailcoat and an old Garibaldi hat, green with age.

He glanced at the corpse.

"Crushed eyeballs," he growled, ". . . again. It's starting to look like an epidemic. It's almost a ritual." He seemed to notice DeKok for the first time.

"Sorry, DeKok, I didn't know you're were part of the investigating team. I thought this was being handled by Headquarters."

DeKok shook his head slowly.

"No longer. As of now it's my case. The Chief Constable has weighed the matter and, in his wisdom, has made his decision."

"They decided to try an old work-horse, eh?" smiled Dr. Koning. "Scraping the bottom of the barrel, what?" The old man could be sarcastic at times.

DeKok was slightly irritated when he answered.

"I'm not an old horse," he reprimanded, "and I wasn't at the bottom of a barrel." Then his good humor got the better of him. "If it had been the bottom of a good bottle of cognac, now, that might have made a difference."

"I did not mean to give offence," assured the old doctor, "but you and I, let us be realists, we are no longer . . ." There was a hint of regret in his voice. "But such is life," he continued, "children grow up and grown men become old." He gestured toward the corpse on the floor. "Regretfully she will not grow old . . . she is dead."

"Thank you, Dr. Koning," replied DeKok formally. Under the Dutch justice system a person is not officially dead, unless declared dead by a Coroner, or a physician. DeKok was always scrupulous in such matters.

"Brain damage," ventured the Coroner.

DeKok was surprised. The old man seldom offered an opinion regarding the cause of death. Sometimes he could be coaxed into a careful admission, but in general he held, quite rightly in DeKok's opinion, that the cause of death was something to be determined by an official autopsy.

"Brain damage?" repeated DeKok.

The old Coroner nodded.

"Fracture of the right *os temporale*, the right temple, resulting in extensive trauma, damage, you understand, of the brains." He hesitated. "Just like the other women," he added

48

reluctantly. "You will find that Dr. Rusteloos will confirm my diagnosis."

"What about the weapon?"

"No weapon."

The old man was bent on confusing him, thought DeKok.

"No weapon?" he asked with disbelief.

"Unless," the old man answered, "you consider the human hand a weapon."

DeKok looked at the old man for several seconds and started to shake his head. Then his lips pressed together in a determined line and he nodded to himself.

"Yes, I do," said DeKok after a long pause. "The human hand ... combined with a devilish intelligence ... the most horrible weapon known to man."

Dr. Koning shook his head.

"You're much too cynical," he chided, surprising DeKok again. "A hand is also used to caress." Then he shrugged his shoulders. "But perhaps you are correct. You do deal, after all, with homicide and that is a cynical business."

He lifted his old Garibaldi hat in a polite gesture, reminiscent of an earlier age, and took his leave. At the door he turned around.

"Good luck, my friend," he said earnestly.

DeKok nodded absent-mindedly. That was the third person to wish him "Good Luck" within the last thirty minutes. He began to believe he needed it. He motioned toward the morgue attendants.

They approached, unfolded their stretcher and with a minimum of wasted movements, they soon had the corpse ready for transport.

Vledder came away from the dresser against which he had been leaning.

"It feels strange not having the *Herd* around," he commented.

Thundering Herd was DeKok's special name for the small army of experts, technical people and assorted bigwigs that always gathered at the scene of a violent death. This time, thanks to the special instructions of the Chief Constable, DeKok had been able to dispense with the crowd. If at all possible he preferred to work with Vledder and the possible assistance of Weelen and Kruger. Over the years he had learned to respect the professionalism and discreet competence of the police photographer and his counter-part in the fingerprint department. The rest of the *Herd* was just wasted time and manpower in DeKok's opinion. If he did need extra assistance, he could always count on the voluntary assistance of a number of young detectives at his own Warmoes Street station. Especially Robert Antoine Dijk and Prins were always eager to work with the famous old sleuth.

"They can go over everything later," growled DeKok. "I just didn't want them underfoot at this time. They've been stamping their flat feet over eight previous killings without result. They can wait. What have *you* got so far?"

Vledder spread out a bunch of papers on the table.

"This is all I found," he said.

"Anything that can help us?" asked DeKok.

"I don't think so," said the young man, shaking his head. "Just the usual stuff . . . insurance policies, hospitalization card, passport, birth announcements, death announcements, photos, bills and some old letters."

"What's her name?"

Vledder picked up the passport.

"Anna Henrietta Deel," he read. "Born in Castricum, twenty-seven years ago." He showed the passport picture to DeKok. "That's her, I think." With a careless movement he threw the passport back on the table. "There are some letters addressed to a 'Mrs. Rozeblad'. There's an old name plate on the door with the same name."

"Married?"

"As far as I've been able to determine, she's divorced. Most of the bills are addressed to Deel, not Rozeblad."

"In that case she must have been married to a Rozeblad," smiled DeKok.

"Exactly."

"Children?"

Vledder pointed at the sideboard.

"There's a whole drawer full of baby pictures and children's pictures. A boy and a girl. But that could be children of family, or acquaintances . . . nieces, nephews."

DeKok nodded pensively. Again he let his gaze roam around the room. To the left of the large sideboard was a big-screen TV of the latest model. To the right, in a corner, a small wet-bar had been installed. Also obviously new. The gray sleuth went into the direction of the bar, stepping over the puddle of blood on the carpet.

He looked at the display behind the bar. Much to his surprise he discovered a bottle of fine French cognac of a brand he preferred above all others. Momentarily his thoughts drifted away to the intimate little bar of his friend Little Lowee.

Suddenly the door opened and slammed against the wall. A young woman stood in the door opening, dressed in a jean suit. She looked flustered and wild. She used one of the door stiles for support while she wiped long, blonde hair out of her face. Her bright green eyes looked fearful and dazed.

"She's dead," she panted. She nodded emphatically, as if to confirm her own words. "I knew it . . . she's dead."

Slowly DeKok came away from the bar. He stopped in front of her and cocked his head.

"Who are you?"

She darted a look at his face, pulled her head between her shoulders like a scared sparrow.

"Josie," she said, still in a daze, "Josephine Ardenwood."

"You . . . eh, you knew the victim?"

She nodded and bit her lower lip with a set of strong, white teeth.

"Yes," she whispered, "Anna . . . Anna Deel, my friend."

DeKok pulled back the sleeve of his jacket and studied his watch with elaborate casualness.

"How did you find out about her death so soon? Who told you?"

"Nobody?"

"Nobody?" marveled DeKok. "You just . . . *knew*?"

5

DeKok took her by the arm and led her into the room.

"We must have a talk," he said in a friendly tone of voice.

Josephine Ardenwood did not seem to hear him. Her eyes darted restlessly around the room.

"Where did you find her?" she asked with a shiver in her voice.

The old detective pointed in the direction of the sofa.

"There," he said softly. "It wasn't a pleasant sight."

"Did they . . ." She took her head between her hands, hiding her face. "Did they do something to her?"

"What do you mean?"

"Has she been raped?"

"Raped?" DeKok was unable to keep a hint of amazement out of his voice. Rape, although not unknown, is a rare crime in the Netherlands. Prostitutes are too readily available for many would-be rapists to chance long jail sentences for something they can obtain for a small price.

"Yes." She nodded emphatically. "Raped."

The gray sleuth slowly shook his head.

"There are no indications," he said slowly, carefully, "that something like that happened." He looked at her. "Did . . . eh, did you expect that?"

She turned to him, a wild look in her eyes.

"There has to be *some* sense to it. All these horrible murders. Obviously it's the work of a sexual maniac." Her voice rose, broke into a sob. "A . . . a beast!"

"In other words . . . a *man*," said DeKok calmly.

She pressed her well-shaped lips together and snorted. There was contempt in the green eyes.

"Of course," she said sharply, "a man. Women don't commit excesses like that."

DeKok ignored the remark. He gently pushed her in the direction of the bar and placed her on a stool.

"How long have you known Anna Deel?"

She looked at the ceiling, a thoughtful look on her face.

"About three months. I first met her in Warmoes Street, at the day-care center where we took our children."

"Anna had children?"

"Two, just like me."

"They're still at the day-care center?"

She shook her head.

"No, no longer. For the last month the children are being taken care of by a nice family in Brabant,* on a farm."

"Why?"

She took her purse and looked for cigarettes, nervously with quick, darting fingers.

"Why?" repeated DeKok. "Were you and Anna afraid something would happen to the children?"

She looked up, absent-mindedly.

"No, of course not. But it was too difficult with the day-care center. You had to get up real early to take the children. In the

---

* Brabant (actually North-Brabant to distinguish it from the province by the same name in Belgium) is a province in the south of the Netherlands.

afternoon you had to be exactly on time. And all in all you're only rid of them for a few hours."

"Hardly worth the trouble," mocked DeKok.

She seemed not to notice the sarcasm.

"And then," she went on, "every time you ran the risk of meeting your ex-husband and there would be all sorts of arguments about the children. Anna and I had had enough."

"You're divorced?"

"Yes," she said. A sad expression fled across her face. "Just like Anna. Almost a year. We both sort of had the same experiences. That's why we were so attracted to each other."

DeKok nodded his understanding.

"You found a soul-mate?"

"Exactly," she said with a wan smile. "That's exactly it . . . a friend . . . a soul-mate."

DeKok looked at her intently, leaned slightly forward.

"You were so much in tune with her that you knew immediately something had happened to her?"

The faint smile around her lips froze. An alert, suspicious look came into her eyes.

"No," she said unwillingly, "that was because of the phone call."

"What sort of phone call?"

"About an hour ago, at home. The phone rang, I picked it up and a voice said: 'Go see what happened to Anna Deel'."

"A male voice?"

She shrugged her shoulders.

"I . . . I think so . . . it *sounded* like a man's voice." She reflected. "It did sound a bit strange, as if it had been taped and run off at a slower speed."

"Did you recognize the voice?"

She made a helpless gesture.

"For a moment I thought it was Charles."

"Charles?"

She covered her face with her hands.

"Anna's ex-husband."

* * *

From New Side Maelstrom they walked back into the direction of Warmoes Street. On the way they passed the beautifully preserved *Korenmetershuis* on New Dike. The Korenmeters–huis, literally *corn measurer's house*, as the name implies, is a corn merchants guild house and was used as such until the late 17th Century. Over the years New Dike (*Nieuwendijk*), so called because it is a mere three hundred years old has changed into a busy shopping street. The pavement gleamed in the rain and reflected the light from the many shop windows. DeKok pushed his hat further into his eyes and pulled up the collar of his coat. His face was somber. The fact that so many had worked on the case before him, made him feel uncomfortable. Why would he succeed when so many had failed? He certainly was not arrogant enough to think that he was more qualified for the job than his colleagues. Certainly not. He glanced at Vledder who easily paced him.

"We still have the problem of the naked lady."

Vledder obviously had been thinking of other things.

"What can we do about it?" he asked, surprise in his voice.

"Please keep in mind," answered DeKok indirectly, "That we came upon the naked lady because of our research into the background of Sylvie Rebergen."

"And you think there's a connection?"

"I think," said DeKok slowly, "that one of the reasons we're involved in the case at this time ... is because we happened to find Sylvie on our own. The other victims were only found after an anonymous phone call . . . something like: go and see there and there and you'll find that and that."

"Like Anna Deel?"

"Yes, Headquarters received a call about Sylvie, shortly after we found the body."

"So, we were ahead of the killer . . ."

"A Phyrus victory," grimaced DeKok.

They walked on in silence.

"What was your opinion of Josie Ardenwood?" asked DeKok after a long silence.

"You should have arrested her," growled the young Inspector.

"Arrested?"

"Yes, at least take her to the station."

"To Warmoes Street?" DeKok was astonished.

"Of course."

"But why?"

Vledder snorted and wiped the rain from his face.

"Because I don't trust her," he said sharply. He stopped in front of DeKok and raised his hands in a dramatic gesture. "In the afternoon," he scoffed, "our Precious Josie gets an alarming telephone call concerning her *soul-mate*, Anna. And what does she do?" There was venom in his voice as he answered his own question. "Nothing, absolutely nothing. She doesn't alert anyone . . . no neighbors, no friends, no police. She waits until evening, several hours later and then she suddenly runs, runs mind you, in a panic to New Side Maelstrom to see if something, after all, may have happened to her *soul-mate*." Vledder grimaced. "And you ask me to believe that . . . that, *tripe*?"

DeKok smiled and started moving again. The somber look had left his face.

"But who says you have to believe it?" he asked with a twinkle in his eye.

59

They crossed Old Bridge Alley and from there traversed the Damrak. DeKok glanced at the Stock Exchange, the forerunner of the New York Stock Exchange. Vledder had told him that many financial principles used in America today were pioneered in the old building. DeKok had no reason to doubt it. Vledder was seldom wrong about that sort of details.

They entered Warmoes Street. As usual Warmoes Street presented a scene of barely controlled chaos. Young tourists, burdened by heavy rucksacks wended their way to a Youth Hostel, B-Girls protected their hair with newspapers as they tried to entice the passers-by into bars. Prostitutes had donned transparent plastic raincoats. It seemed as if the raincoats made them bolder than usual. A few wore only a G-string under the coat and some not even that. An addict leaned against a facade and stared into the distance, oblivious to the world around him. Two sailors were seated cross-legged in the middle of the street, amicably sharing a bottle of liquor. Vledder took time out to direct them to the sidewalk. They cheerfully complied with his polite request and were soon sitting on the edge of the pavement, across from the police station. A tramp joined in and they peacefully passed the bottle between the three of them.

The two Inspectors climbed the worn bluestone steps toward the station. A gray desk-sergeant spoke in a fatherly tone to a young girl who had apparently run away from home. He interrupted his advice when he saw Vledder and DeKok. He motioned them over to the desk and gave them a large, yellow envelope.

"For you," he said, "dropped off by some guys from Headquarters."

They passed through the railing that separated the public part of the station from the restricted area and hoisted themselves up the old marble stairs to the second floor. In the large detective room DeKok tossed his hat at the coat rack and missed, as usual.

With a grin he picked up his hat and hung it next to his dripping raincoat.

Vledder took the envelope and looked at the impressive seals.

"Should I open it?" he asked, since the envelope was addressed to DeKok.

"Sure," nodded DeKok. "But I know what's in it . . . the files on the previous murders." He sat down behind his desk. "I don't plan to read any of it."

Vledder was only mildly surprised. DeKok was well known for his abhorrence of reports. If he read any reports at all, they were usually Vledder's reports. Even then, he much preferred to have the contents summarized for him. And that too, happened infrequently.

"But don't you want to know what happened before?" asked Vledder. "Maybe it will help if we know what has been accomplished so far."

DeKok raked a hand through his hair.

"I don't want to know."

"Why not?"

"I prefer to go my own way."

Vledder tried once more. He slapped his hand on the heavy envelope.

"But extremely competent policemen have worked on these files," he said. "For more than half a year."

DeKok nodded. His face was serious and his tone resigned.

"That's exactly why I don't want to see it. There will be no loose ends in the files. I'm sure that they have done everything possible to find the killer . . . every lead has been followed, every hint has been researched . . . in detail, as usual."

Vledder was getting obdurate.

"These terrible murders have certain clear characteristics," he argued. "They're recognizable. In our investigations we will, no doubt, encounter the same sets of circumstances. And what they have already checked, we don't have . . ."

DeKok interrupted, waved away the stream of words.

"Then we'll investigate all over again," he said curtly.

Vledder took the envelope and with a wild gesture broke the seals.

"But I *will* read it," he said stubbornly. "Every letter."

* * *

The phone on DeKok's desk rang. After several rings, when DeKok made no move to answer it, Vledder leaned forward and lifted the receiver. He looked up after a few seconds.

"There's a Mr. Rozeblad downstairs."

"Let him come up," sighed DeKok.

The man who entered the detective room was big, wide, almost colossal, with long arms and enormous feet. Hesitantly he waited just inside the door. A detective pointed out DeKok's desk. He approached and stood in front of the desk, strangely tense, almost at attention. A shy smile seemed to hover around his thick lips. He gave the impression that he was trying to apologize for his presence, or perhaps for the large amount of space he required.

DeKok had risen from his chair and looked the man up and down. The man looked unkempt. The gray suit was spotted and did not fit right. His tie was loose, his shirt was wrinkled and there was a greasy ring inside his collar.

"Rozeblad?"

The man nodded.

"Charles . . . Charles Rozeblad."

DeKok stretched out his hand and showed a friendly smile. With a courteous gesture he indicated the chair next to his desk.

"Please sit down," he said, as the man sank down in the chair. "My name is DeKok." He gestured toward Vledder. "This is my colleague, Dick Vledder." He stared at the man for a few seconds. The smile faded from his face and he looked serious when he continued. ""Our condolences on the loss of your . . . eh, your ex-wife."

Charles Rozeblad nodded curtly. He produced a large handkerchief from his pocket and wiped his sweaty forehead.

"Where are my kids?" he asked brusquely.

"Children?" asked DeKok with well-feigned surprise.

The man nodded vehemently. The shyness had disappeared.

"I have two kids, a boy and a girl." A tender smile transformed his puffy face. "Wonderful kids, real darlings. I'm especially attached to the boy." He fell silent, shook his head. "She squirreled them away, the bitch, kept them from me. I haven't seen them for months."

"Why did she do that?"

"What?"

"Keep the children from you," clarified DeKok impatiently.

"She used them as leverage, you see, in order to get her way. By keeping the children away from me, she has forced me to increase the alimony three times." He pressed his lips together, shook his head again. A few drops of sweat splattered the edge of DeKok's desk. "Three times," he added, "in less than two years. She knew I love the kids."

"Moral blackmail."

"Blackmail, that's the word." Rozeblad seemed to embrace it eagerly. "That's exactly the word for it. Blackmail. Pure and simple blackmail and nobody does anything about it. You can go to Social Services, the Juvenile Protection Agency, the Court, you can do what you want, but it's all for nought." His voice was bitter. "A man is powerless in that sort of situation."

The gray sleuth shook his head.

"I agree with you, you have your rights as well. You should have agreed on a binding agreement, binding for both parties."

Charles Rozeblad reacted violently. He threw his arms up in the air and gesticulated. His face became red.

"I tried," he exclaimed. "God knows I tried . . . again and again. But I always gave in, gave in to her demands." He lowered his arms and seemed to calm down a little. "Only this afternoon," he went on, "I wanted Anna to, I wanted to . . ." He stopped suddenly. His eyes became wide and his mouth fell open. There was a sly look in his eyes as he looked at DeKok.

DeKok had not missed the by-play, the hesitation, the sudden change in attitude.

"What did you want this afternoon, Mr. Rozeblad?" he asked softly.

The man remained silent. He swallowed and again wiped his forehead with the large handkerchief. DeKok leaned closer.

"What, Mr. Rozeblad?" he insisted.

Rozeblad persisted in his silence. His tongue licked along dry lips, his eyes evaded DeKok and sweat beaded his forehead. DeKok leaned closer still, the fleshy face of Rozeblad was very near. An artery throbbed nervously in his neck.

"I'll tell you," whispered DeKok confidentially. "You wanted to talk to Anna, reasonably, like intelligent adults. You were hoping for understanding, tried to make it clear to her that they were your children as well. But Anna didn't want to listen, laughed at you, said that as far as she was concerned, you'd *never* see the children again."

The gray sleuth paused, took a deep breath and gauged the reactions on the face in front of him.

"Then you became angry," he whispered again. "You felt the anger get the best of you and suddenly you realized how much you hated her, how she had destroyed your life, had stolen all the joy from your life . . . and when she laughed again . . . again said that . . ."

Rozeblad jumped up. His chair clattered against the floor.

"No," he called out, stretching out his hands as if to push away an imaginary foe. "No . . . you're crazy . . . not me. I didn't kill her."

DeKok rose and straightened out to his full height. His face was a pitiless mask. He walked around the desk and approached the man. Despite the man's enormous size, he seemed to shrink in front of DeKok's eyes. He became smaller, almost cowering in his fear. He shook his head again and again.

"She was already dead . . . she was already dead."

6

"She was already dead!"

Rozeblad's cry bounced off the walls of the detective room. Several detectives looked up, smiled and then shrugged. DeKok had another of his dramatic visitors. It was almost a regular occurrence. DeKok took the man by the arm and led him back to the desk. With one hand he righted the chair.

"Sit down," he said sharply. "So, you were there?"

"Yes."

"Why?"

Charles Rozeblad searched his pockets and came out with a wrinkled envelope which he placed on DeKok's desk.

"Her lawyer wrote me to say she wanted to talk to me."

"When?"

"This afternoon, at her house."

"What time?"

"Two o'clock."

"And you were on time?"

"Maybe a few minutes late," nodded Rozeblad. "But not much later. I parked the car about a block away, near Front Fort Canal, at a meter. I walked from there. I was in no hurry. I was trying to gather my thoughts, planning what I was going to say to her."

"Any idea what she wanted to talk about?"

Rozeblad grinned joylessly.

"Money, what else? Anna had a hole in her hand. She spent money like water, unwisely, sometimes just to buy dubious friends." He paused. "She never understood, or didn't *want* to understand, that I had to work hard for every penny." He sighed deeply. "She couldn't have cared less."

DeKok studied him, listened to the bitter tone.

"You were ready to kill," he observed evenly.

Rozeblad lowered his head, stared at the floor.

"To be honest," he said softly, "the thought of murder has gone through my mind, once or twice. There was no way I could have gone on like this for the rest of my life."

DeKok sat back. He never trusted a person who started a sentence with "to be honest". It always made him feel, that honesty was such a rare quality in a person that they had to emphasize it when they were supposedly "honest". Even then, experience had taught him, they usually lied. He wondered what Rozeblad was lying about. The number of times he had *thought* about murder, or that he could not go on? At the same time he was almost convinced that the man had not killed his ex-wife. Where would be the connection with the other victims? DeKok rubbed his face with both hands.

"So," he said wearily, "it was just a happy accident of fate that somebody else had done the killing for you?"

Rozeblad moved in his chair. He looked up and his eyes flashed. The weak mouth hardened.

"I have nothing to do with her death," he said. The reaction was sharp, emotional. "Nothing, you hear me. And you're not going to convince me that I did."

DeKok smiled mildly.

"I'm looking for the truth," he said calmly, soothingly. "It's the nature of my business." He made an apologetic gesture. "Did you touch anything in the house?"

"No," denied Rozeblad. "I saw almost at once that she was dead."

"How?"

"The way she was laying there, her position . . . the blood on her face."

"Then what?"

"Nothing. Not a thing. I was paralyzed, too astonished to do anything. I don't know how long I stood there, as if frozen. When I was again able to move, I ran into the street. My only thought was to get away. I vaguely remember bumping into people. Eventually I found a bar, somewhere at Martyr's Canal. I had a couple of stiff drinks. It helped. It helped to revive me, so to speak."

"And then you called Josie Ardenwood from the bar?"

The surprise on Rozeblad's face seemed genuine.

"I called who?"

"Josie . . . Josephine Ardenwood, Anna's friend."

Rozeblad shook his head in bewilderment.

"I . . . I didn't call anybody."

Again DeKok took the time to study the man. Then he stood up.

"You may go," he said tonelessly.

Hesitating, Charles Rozeblad rose from his chair.

"And what about my kids?"

"According to my information, they have been taken to Brabant. They live with a good family, on a farm. As soon as I have the address, I'll contact you."

The large man swallowed.

"You . . . eh, I mean, . . . eh, I'm no longer a suspect?"

DeKok grinned crookedly.

"If I find enough evidence against you . . . I'll come and pick you up in person."

Rozeblad shook his head slowly.

"You won't find anything against me. *That* assurance I can give you."

With slumped shoulders he turned around and walked away. DeKok stared after him. As soon as the door had closed behind the man, DeKok turned to Vledder.

"Have you arranged about the autopsy?"

"Of course."

"Fine, let me know what happens."

"You're not coming?"

"No," said DeKok, shaking his head. "I'm going to Bloemendaal tomorrow."

"Why Bloemendaal?"

DeKok gave him a tired smile.

"That's where I'll find the sorrowing widow of the late Professor Dinterloo. Perhaps she'll know something about the naked lady."

* * *

DeKok drove slowly and carefully, only occasionally grinding the gears. With Vledder at the autopsy and the public transportation connections to the small town of Bloemendaal what they were, he had no choice. He detested driving and knew he was probably one of the worst drivers in Europe, certainly in Holland. It had been a minor miracle when he finally, after more than a dozen attempts, had passed the driving test. The theory was fine and he had no trouble with the traffic laws, but it always seemed as if the vehicles sensed his dislike of all things mechanical and did everything in their power to make life miserable for him. Which, of course, intensified his dislike even more.

Instead of driving straight to Bloemendaal, he had decided to avoid the heavily traveled routes and had chosen the scenic route along the coast near Zandvoort. In addition to being a favorite resort town for Amsterdammers, it was also the site of one of the most demanding car-racing tracks in the world. DeKok knew that, but immediately dismissed it from his mind as he saw the inviting beach. For just a moment he contemplated going for a swim. But he had not brought any trunks and his puritanical soul would not allow him to enjoy the beach *au naturel*. Which did not prevent him from enjoying the sight of the lithe, bronzed bodies on the beach. With a sigh of regret he turned off the Sea Road and entered the village proper.

He parked, badly, on a wide thoroughfare and proceeded on foot toward Rose Lane. He stared at the rich houses like any tourist. The Bloemendaal-Aerdenhout area is, after Wassenaar, the most affluent community of the Netherlands. Before he realized it he found himself in front of 387 Rose Lane. It was a pompous villa with large windows and a lot of polished woodwork. He touched the brass door-knocker and heard a faint "ding-dong" in the interior of the house. After a few minutes the door was opened by a young woman. DeKok recognized her immediately from the funeral. He noticed that close-up she was just as attractive as he had remembered. Not a wild, exotic beauty, but calm, simple, with a certain grace and reserve that so often masked a passionate nature. She looked at him.

"Inspector DeKok?" she asked.

DeKok nodded and she gave him her hand in a spontaneous gesture.

"Marianne Dinterloo," she introduced herself.

DeKok pressed the offered hand and became aware of the firm, muscled grace.

"My condolences on the loss of your husband," he said formally.

She gave him a grateful nod. Then she led the way down a long corridor that ended in a spacious room where a small child played with some dolls. She indicated some easy chairs.

"Please have a seat," she said.

She sat down across from him, her legs primly together, the skirt pulled down over the knees. She stared at DeKok for a few seconds.

"You were at the funeral?"

"With my colleague, Vledder," admitted DeKok.

"May I ask whether you have a professional interest in my husband's death?"

DeKok pursed his lips.

"You may," he said finally.

"Do you?"

"Yes."

"In that case, may I ask on what grounds you have based your professional interest? I mean, was my husband the victim of a crime?"

The gray sleuth hesitated, wiped his face with a broad hand. He did not like it when others asked the questions.

"Somebody delivered the death announcement to me," he said after a long pause.

"And?"

"I thought the text a bit . . . eh, unusual."

She looked him full in the face, an alert look in her eyes.

"What was unusual about it?"

DeKok scratched the back of his neck.

"Your husband drove his car into the canal. In the Announcement it mentioned 'a brief suffering'. It's not exactly common usage in a case like that." He paused. "And," he went on, "the request for no crocuses, or other flowers . . ." He paused again, leaned closer. "Did *you* pick the text, Mrs. Dinterloo?"

A hint of emotion broke through the serene self-possession of the attractive woman. Her lower lip quivered ever so slightly.

"No, not mine, not my choice . . . my husband's."

"Your husband wrote his own death announcement?"

"Shortly before he died."

"And you didn't think that strange?"

She adjusted her skirt which did not need adjusting.

"Fred wasn't very happy, the last few months. He was nervous, restless, talked about death as a way out." She shook her head. "He should have stayed in Twente."

"He didn't like it at ITO?"

She sighed deeply.

"Fred wasn't the sort of man for intrigues, office politics, constant juggling for power. He was a man of science, who wanted to work in a calm, quiet atmosphere . . . a pure researcher."

"Surely that was possible at Tropic Oil?"

She gave him a sad smile.

"In fact, he had little personal freedom. Everybody in management tried to use him for his, or her, own purposes . . . *mis*-use him, I should say. He felt threatened from all sides." She lowered her head, a sad tone came into her voice. "And then there was that woman," she added softly.

"What woman?"

"Diana Gellecom."

DeKok's eyebrows rippled in that sudden movement of which they were capable. Vledder would have studied the phenomenon with interest. Mrs. Dinterloo, too, seemed momentarily fascinated. She blinked her eyes, as if to clear her vision, but by then the eyebrows had returned to their normal, albeit somewhat bushy, appearance.

"You're talking about the wife of the CEO?"

She nodded slowly.

"A terrible woman ... power-hungry, irresponsible and scandalous. She tried all sorts of tricks to make my husband fall into her trap, her clutches. No means were too foul. The Gellecoms have a beautiful house near the lake, with a magnificent garden. When we were invited she was unable to suppress her affections for my husband. Didn't care, more likely." She smoothed her hair. "Fred wasn't strong enough to withstand that. He was helpless in that sort of situation. In many ways he was very naive, had a childlike quality."

"And what about Gellecom himself?"

Mrs. Dinterloo shrugged her shapely shoulders.

"I don't think Max cared. He has reconciled himself to his wife's behavior. When I remarked on it once, he said something about her still being young, still needing to live out her fantasies." She made a hesitant gesture. "Perhaps he has little choice. Max is at least thirty years older than his wife."

DeKok nodded his understanding. Meanwhile he continued to study the woman. The almond shaped eyes, the ivory shade of her skin and her delicate bones gave her a fragile beauty. DeKok realized that this was a woman who would become more beautiful with time, a woman who was truly one of the "beautiful people". He leaned toward her.

"Who is the Naked Lady?" he asked suddenly.

She looked at him with surprise.

"Naked lady?" she repeated, confused.

DeKok nodded.

"Ask for the naked lady. It was written on a card that had been stuck under the wipers of our car when we left the cemetery. A pink card from *Casa Erotica*."

"The sex-club?"

"You know about it?" DeKok was scandalized.

74

She shook her head with a reassuring smile, as if guessing his thoughts.

"Fred was there once, with some people from Tropic Oil. That was about two days before he died."

DeKok pulled at his lower lip and let it plop back. He seemed unaware of the annoying sound he created. He repeated the unsavory gesture several times.

"What time did he come home that night?" he asked finally.

"He never did come home that night," she answered. "He didn't come home until late in the morning. He seemed relieved, less tense. He told me that he had gotten drunk and that he had a big fight with Max Gellecom. Some girl took him home to her apartment."

"Sylvie Rebergen."

"Yes," agreed Marianne Dinterloo, "that was her name. Fred showed me. He had written her name and address on one of those pink cards from Casa Erotica. According to Fred she was a sweet girl with a lot of understanding." She smiled indulgently. "Apparently they talked all night."

DeKok listened carefully, watched her expression, analyzed the tone of voice. He was looking for undertones of revenge, hate, or jealousy. But she was refreshingly guileless. "Sylvie is also dead," he said.

She nodded. A tear pinked in the corner of an almond-shaped eye.

"I read it in the papers," she said with a broken voice. "Poor girl. Murdered." She lifted her head, impatiently wiped away the tears from her eyes. "Just like my husband?"

DeKok felt a lump in his throat. The quiet, dignified sorrow of the young woman touched him. He glanced at the child who played quietly with her dolls.

"I have no real evidence that your husband was murdered," he said soberly. "But I *would* like to know what your husband discussed with Sylvie, that night."

Marianne Dinterloo suddenly reacted tensely. The sad, reminiscent look disappeared and was replaced with an expression of hate and disgust.

"I know," she said tautly. "I know what they talked about . . . they talked about Diana . . . Diana Gellecom . . . she wanted Fred to divorce me."

"In order to marry her?"

"Exactly."

"But she was already married."

"Fred told her the same thing."

"And then?"

Marianne looked at him. There was astonishment in her eyes.

"Diana said it didn't matter . . . Max would die in a few weeks."

DeKok rubbed the corners of his eyes. He had trouble absorbing the sudden mood-swings of the young woman. Her attractiveness helped to confuse him, made it more difficult to focus on the important aspects of the interview. With some difficulty he rose from his easy chair. He looked down on her.

"That night," he asked softly, "the night that Fred drove into the canal and drowned . . . did he come from the Gellecom house?"

Marianne lifted her face to him. The hate had disappeared and made room for a mild, tolerant expression. She nodded slowly.

"Yes. He went to tell her that he was through with her. That he never wanted to see her again."

It sounded like a fulfilled prophecy.

* * *

DeKok gave his young partner a penetrating look.

"How was the autopsy?"

Vledder shrugged his wide shoulders.

"Dr. Rusteloos seemed a bit depressed, discouraged. According to him he might as well have made a photocopy of his previous reports. All he had to do was change the name."

"He found the same cause of death as in the other cases, I take it?"

Vledder nodded dejectedly.

"Yes. Lethal brain damage, fracture of the skull and the eyes crushed." He shook his head. "Now I know why you didn't want to come along. It wasn't a pretty sight."

"Was there anything special about her?"

"What do you mean?"

"Physical characteristics," said DeKok, irked. "Anything that set her apart."

"Anna Deel," smiled Vledder, "was exceptionally beautiful. Well proportioned, long legs, slender waist, a perfect bust line . . . even Dr. Rusteloos remarked on her beauty."

DeKok waved impatiently.

"And what about the other eight? Were they also beauty queens?" There was biting irony in his voice.

Vledder gave his mentor an amused look.

"I thought you didn't want to know about the files?"

The gray sleuth looked embarrassed. He rubbed the bridge of his nose with a little finger and avoided Vledder's eyes.

"Ah . . . well, . . . eh, *you* read it, didn't you?" he evaded.

"Yes, and it took some time. It took me more than three hours to plow through it all and I *still* don't have all the details firmly in my mind." He reached into an inside pocket and placed his notebook in front of him, "I made a little list for myself," he continued, ". . . about the victims. Things like name, age, skin color, hair color, eyes, education, financial situation . . . that sort of thing. I put it all in the computer and let it do its thing."

"And?"

Vledder waved his notebook in the air.

"I can understand the despair of the guys at Headquarters. No matter which way you try to fit it together, there is just no common thread."

"All that was in the files?"

"No, not everything. There was a list, of course, but it just contained names, birth dates, time of death, you know."

"And there was no line there?"

"No."

"How did you get the additional information, like financial stuff and so?"

"Thanks to Miss Graven."

"And who," asked DeKok, "is Miss Graven?"

"A social worker," smiled Vledder secretively.

"And what does a social worker have to do with the murders?"

"A lot, quite a lot, as a matter of fact. She wrote a report on most of the victims."

"Why?"

"Because the victims asked for help regarding child support." The young Inspector moved his chair closer to DeKok's desk. "Miss Graven," he explained patiently, "works for social services, but she's also a sort of liaison with Juvenile Protection. She also oversees requests for financial help and that way she became familiar with most of the victims. Headquarters has interrogated her exhaustively."

"Did all the victims need financial assistance? You did say 'most', didn't you?"

"Yes I did and no, not all of them came into contact with Miss Graven and her department. Some were well able to take care of themselves, could even be called well-off. But most of them were entitled to some sort of financial support. Some were being paid directly by social services, pending a decision of the court regarding alimony, or child support and others had trouble collecting the amounts assigned by the courts."

"Courts," said DeKok, irritation in his voice. "Alimony?"

"Yes. There's one thing all the victims have in common."

"So?"

"Yes, *all* of them either were divorced, or just about to be divorced."

"*All* of them? All eight?"

"All nine."

"You're right, all nine. Anna Deel was divorced as well." DeKok paused, looked at his young friend. "Coincidence?" he asked.

Vledder shook his head emphatically.

"No, I think it's a factor. It's too obvious."

The gray sleuth rested his head in his hands and stared into the distance. For a long time he did not say anything. Then he stood up, ambled over to the coat rack and placed his hat on his head.

Vledder followed him.

"Where are you going?"

DeKok grinned brightly.

"I'm going to see Lowee. I think that a cognac is the only thing that can help me at this point."

7

Lowee the barkeeper, for obvious reasons called "Little" Lowee, wiped his hands hastily on the towel he had wrapped around his waist. With a happy smile he reached over the bar and shook DeKok's hand. No matter how often DeKok came to the bar, Lowee was always happy to see him and always greeted him like a long-lost friend. He pointed at Vledder.

"You done brung the young gennelman with you, I see."

DeKok smiled in return while he hoisted himself on a stool.

"It's about time he learns a *good* habit," he joked.

The barkeeper nodded solemn agreement. The eyes in the friendly, mousy face twinkled. Then he dived under the bar and emerged almost immediately with a bottle he kept especially for DeKok's visits. With the same, rapid movements he placed three large snifters next to the bottle. He gave DeKok a few seconds to admire the label and then he held up the bottle.

"Same recipe?" he asked, as he always did. Without waiting for an answer he poured the precious liquid in the waiting glasses.

Silently the three men lifted their glasses and cradled them, warming the cognac with their hands. Then they carefully tasted the first heavenly sips. Little Lowee and DeKok had repeated this ceremony for many years, two, three times, or oftener per week. The men had grown close over the years, the ceremony had become something exalted, an important part of their lives.

Vledder was the first to put his glass back on the bar. He still lacked the calm, the patience for reflection that was part of enjoying a good glass of cognac. To DeKok it was never just the drink . . . it was the ambiance, the aroma, the ritual, the companionship. They were all part of a good glass of cognac. Sometimes he missed the cigars he used to smoke. Even to this day, although he had not smoked for more than ten years, he still felt that a cigar with a glass of cognac could hardly be described as mere smoking. Both DeKok and Lowee looked mildly at Vledder as he placed his glass on the counter.

"I don't like habits," said Vledder obstinately. "Habits lead to rote and that leads to a rut."

DeKok shook his head sadly and Lowee shook his head in commiseration. Both men were saddened by Vledder's remark. Surely, they thought, that might apply to *some* circumstances, but certainly did *not* include the time hallowed imbibing of cognac. To them Vledder's remark sounded like sacrilege. The cop and the petty criminal, because that was Lowee's other occupation, thought alike in those matters.

"Every person has certain traditions," said DeKok in a didactic tone of voice. "Habits that are dear to him, or her. Sometimes they form the very foundation of life. Habits can be useful. Just think about our killer, you discovered it yourself . . . he only kills divorced women."

"You can hardly call that a habit," began Vledder heatedly.

"Then what would you call it?"

"An aberration, a disease, a maniacal obsession."

Lowee entered the discussion. Carefully he placed his glass on the bar and turned toward DeKok.

"Did you get the death ticket all right?" he asked curiously.

"Death ticket?" asked DeKok, evading the question.

"Exactum," affirmed Lowee cheerfully. "Inna yeller envelope. Little Johnnie, the kid from next door, was gonna drop it orf at the station."

DeKok swallowed.

"You," he exclaimed, taken aback, "you had the death announcement delivered to the station?" There was so much astonishment and disbelief in his voice that it shocked the small barkeeper. He looked at DeKok with wide open eyes, as if he had seen a ghost.

"Y-yep, yes," he stuttered, "me."

"Why?"

"Because she axed me to."

"Who?"

"Sylvie, a girl from the sex-club around the corner. She were afraid to do it herself. Give this card to DeKok, she says, I liketa stay away from them cops."

The gray sleuth rubbed his face and sighed. Then he raised both hands in a gesture of despair.

"Listen, Lowee," he said soothingly. "This is important. Sylvie was here?"

The small barkeeper nodded, completely mystified.

"Sure. She come often. Between shows, so to speak." He pointed. "She always usta sit at the table over there."

"When did she give you the envelope?"

"She never give me no envelope. Just the ticket. She done write something onnit witta pencil." Lowee's gutter language became more pronounced as he became more agitated.

"Did you read it?"

"Yep, something about anuther victim."

"When she gave you the announcement, did she say anything?"

Little Lowee shook his head.

"She ain't tole me nuthing. I just sorta talked to her, you knows, at the bar. She tole me she done gone from the sex-club for a coupla days already. Ain't like it no more. Then when she goes, she gimme one of them pink cards. Put it with the other, she says." The slender barkeeper pointed toward the bottles behind him. "I put it there. I figures you come by an' I give it to you." His face fell. "But you don't show. So, next morning I still sees it there and I put it inna envelope and axed little Johnnie to bring it to you."

"And the card from Casa Erotica?"

"I plum forgot. When I discovers it I went to the station meself, but you're gone already. I figures you gone to the funeral."

"I see," said DeKok without getting angry. He knew how Lowee's mind could work in circles. "So you drove to Sorrow Field and stuck the card under the wiper."

"Exactum," grinned Lowee. "No sweat, I knows your car."

"But why did you not find us and give it to us then?" asked Vledder hotly. "Why so mysterious?"

Lowee spared him a disdainful look.

"I gotta business to run, you knows. Ain't got time to run after cops. Besides," he added with a grin. "DeKok was gonna figure it out anyways."

Vledder looked disgusted and remained silent.

DeKok seemed to have been deep in thought during the exchange, now he addressed Lowee again.

"So, although she didn't give you the two items, the death announcement and the card, at the same time, she *did* give them to you on the same day?"

Lowee became serious.

"Yessir, the day before they found her dead."

DeKok stared at the empty brandy snifter.

"Pour me another one, Lowee, I need it. You're going to turn me into an alcoholic."

"Iffen you ain't already," said Lowee. "You knows what they say, if you ever feels you *needs* a drink, you're an alky."

DeKok looked pensive, but did not stop the barkeeper when he lifted the bottle in order to refill the glasses.

"What about them karate killings?" asked Lowee as he pulled the first glass a little closer.

DeKok suddenly sat up straight. It was the second blow administered by Lowee in the last few minutes.

"Say that again?" he demanded.

"The ka-ra-te killings," repeated Lowee, abashed, intimidated by DeKok's tone.

"Karate killings," repeated DeKok, rolling the words around on his tongue.

"Yep," nodded Lowee, "them strange killings, all them women."

DeKok's eyebrows suddenly seemed to shoot straight out from his head. It was as if he had grown two bushy horns. Lowee gaped at him. He had seen the eyebrows ripple and he had seen a movement that could only be described as dancing, but this was something he had never seen. Then he shook his head. As usual, the phenomenon had disappeared as quickly as it happened and like many people before him, he just was not sure that he had seen what he thought he had seen. Then DeKok's question penetrated as he repeated the question.

"Who calls them karate killings?" repeated the old sleuth.

"The boys," said Lowee, waving vaguely around. "The guys in the neighborhood. They say the women are killed with a karate blow."

"And how did they come to draw *that* conclusion?"

Lowee shrugged his shoulders.

"Aw, come on DeKok, you knows how it is . . . a whisper here, a gossip there . . ."

"Out with it," interrupted DeKok impatiently.

Lowee swallowed.

"Well, all them women lost their eyes and died of a cracked headbone, ain't it?"

"That is karate?"

"I don't know," answered Lowee shyly. "I don't know no karate. But a lotta guys does. It's the latest thing."

"Are you telling me I should look for the killer in this neighborhood,"

A cloud darkened Lowee's face.

"You thinks what you thinks, DeKok," he said stiffly. "I ain't having no part of that."

The gray sleuth grinned. He pointed at the empty glasses.

"You forgot to pour, Lowee . . . the unforgivable barkeeper's sin."

8

"*Shuto gammen-uschi.*"

DeKok laughed.

"What . . . eh, what was that again?"

"*Shuto gammen-uschi*, according to Masutatsu Oyama."

"And who," asked DeKok, "is Masutatsu Oyama?"

Jan VanLooijen smiled pleasantly.

"A Japanese who has written very thick books about karate."

DeKok chewed his lower lip.

"*Shuto gammen-uschi*," he repeated. "So, karate after all."

VanLooijen's face was serious.

"It's one of the 'killing blows', a deadly blow that is administered with lightning speed."

"How?"

Jan VanLooijen took a step back, moved his right hand to almost behind his ear and pushed it forward in a strong, slow-motion movement, the palm up and the fingers slightly bent.

"This way," he explained, "but faster. With the outside metacarpal bone, the connecting rod, so to speak, between the wrist and the little finger. Some practitioners of karate have a

89

highly developed edge on their hand, the bones are as strong as steel."

DeKok nodded his understanding.

"Is there no defense?" he asked. "I mean at one time it was all *jujitsu*, then *judo* and now, apparently, *karate*. I seem to remember that there are various kinds of karate and there's also something else: *king kong*, or *kong king*, or whatever."

VanLooijen laughed.

"*Kung fu*," he corrected. "It's popular because of a lot of so-called 'kung-fu' movies. In Holland a lot of those sports have lagged behind, mostly because of Anton Geesink from Utrecht."

"Oh?"

"Yes, in 1961 Anton Geesink was the first non-Japanese to win the world-championship in Judo, all categories. Then in the 64 Olympic Games in Japan, he took the Gold medal. For decades, judo was *the* popular self-defense sport in Holland. Anton was much admired for his ability in a sport that had always been so dominated by the Japanese."

"Well, could it be used as a defense?"

VanLooijen shrugged his shoulders.

"Karate . . . karate is a fighting sport." He hesitated, thought a moment. "Let me phrase that another way. It's a way of fighting without weapons, but geared for attack . . . to destroy, or render harmless the attacker. *Jujitsu* and *Judo* and most of *kung-fu*, are mainly geared for defense." He shook his head sadly. "Those poor women never had a chance . . . especially not after the preparatory *nihon nukite*."

"Excuse me, but what did you say, neon something?"

Jan VanLooijen demonstrated again.

"*Nihon nukite* is the name of the blow that took their eyes. It happens with an upward motion, as you saw, with the index finger and middle finger pointed forward, slightly spread." He made a contemptuous gesture. "It's rather easy and requires almost no force."

"How long does it all take?"

"You mean a *nihon nukite*, followed by a *shuto gammen-uschi*?"

"Yes."

"A fraction of a second."

DeKok scratched the back of his neck.

"Does everybody who practices karate," he asked suspiciously, "also learn those movements?"

VanLooijen nodded calmly.

"It doesn't exactly happen on the first day, but if they come to my school . . . rather quickly."

DeKok turned around and pointed at about a dozen men who were practicing at the other end of the large room.

"How about them?"

Jan VanLooijen looked past DeKok at the sweating men.

"Most of them," he admitted evenly. "Some are very good."

DeKok rubbed the bridge of his nose with a little finger. This talk was depressing, he thought. He had grown up in a time when a cop needed broad shoulders and a pair of heavy fists. Usually that was enough to quell any disturbance. He had never had to use his nightstick and since he had joined the plain clothed force he had never even carried a weapon. But times changed. He sighed.

"How many people practice karate?"

"In Holland?"

"Yes," said DeKok with a faint smile. "Let's limit it to that."

"Thousands . . . tens of thousands."

"All men?"

Jan VanLooijen shook his head slowly. There was a grin on his face and his dark eyes laughed.

"No, women too. I know a few . . . experts . . . well, let's just say that unless they are explicitly prepared to cooperate, I wouldn't dare bother them."

* * *

From Blood Street they approached Rear Fort Canal. It was busy. The many sex-theaters were operating at top capacity and there seemed more prostitutes in the street than usual. The sexually deprived, or those who thought they were, walked along the sidewalks in droves, looked at the offered excitement and made their choice. Curtains opened and closed with the regularity of a well oiled machine as the prostitutes entertained their clients. There was a queue in front of one of the small hotels that rented rooms by the hour and the raucous music from many bars intermingled with the hundreds of languages being spoken.

Neither Vledder, nor DeKok, took any conscious notice of the crowds around them. Deep in thought they walked on. After a while Vledder looked at DeKok.

"Who's Jan VanLooijen?" he asked.

DeKok did not seem to hear the question. He slowed down a little and waved toward a beautiful woman at the other side of the canal.

"Who's Jan VanLooijen?" repeated Vledder.

"An ex-cop."

"A cop?"

"Extremely active during his time," nodded DeKok. "A professional down to the tips of his fingers."

"Then why," asked Vledder, perplexed, "isn't he on the force any longer. Why a sports school and in Blood Street, of all places."

DeKok smiled.

"Because Jan VanLooijen is of the opinion that as owner, operator and principal instructor of a sports school, he can fight crime a lot more effectively than as a cop . . . especially in *this* neighborhood."

"A lofty ambition," replied Vledder, a sneer in his voice.

"Yes, indeed," agreed DeKok seriously, "I have a lot of admiration for his work."

The young Inspector stopped in the middle of the street.

"I wonder," he ventured, "how far you can go, as an ex-cop . . . I mean, how selective do you have to be?"

"With what?"

"Regarding the people you teach karate."

DeKok looked annoyed.

"What's your problem? I told you: I admire his work. He's very popular, too. Especially the younger people admire him very much."

Vledder did nor respond directly.

"While you were talking to him, I took a peek at the membership list of that school of his. It was just there, on the desk in the office."

"And?"

"Guess who have been students for years?"

"Karate students?"

"Yes, karate."

"No more guessing games, please, out with it."

"Charles Rozeblad . . . and Diana Gellecom."

"What!?"

Vledder nodded slowly to himself.

"Yes. Anna's ex-husband and the lively wife of the Tropic Oil CEO."

* * *

They walked on in silence, each caught in his own circle of thoughts. DeKok felt confused. The discovery that the women had been killed by karate blows had shocked him. It was the first time in his long career as a Homicide detective that he had been confronted with "death by karate". He had seen some demonstrations and the Amsterdam police had even put together a sort of "training" film, edited from a number of Chinese and Japanese fight films. But he had never encountered karate in stark reality, as now. There are definite advantages for the murderer, he thought. The use of a weapon always left a trace. Bullets, shells, powder burns in the case of pistols, or any kind of firearm. Hitting, or stabbing instruments also offered several possibilities for the police. But karate . . .

The gray sleuth interrupted his musings and addressed Vledder.

"Is the name Charles Rozeblad mentioned anywhere in the files of the previous murders?"

Vledder shook his head.

"No, not a hint." He paused and added: "But that's logical. Charles Rozeblad is Anna Deel's ex-husband and *her* murder was not investigated by Headquarters. Just us."

He sounded bitter, but DeKok ignored it.

"What about the other ex-husbands?" he asked evenly.

"Just as a reference," said Vledder nonchalantly. "As a connection with the women from whom they were divorced . . . or about to be divorced."

"That's all? I mean . . . no connections to the other victims?"

Vledder shook his head decisively.

"No. Besides . . . they all had a perfect alibi."

"All eight of them?" DeKok seemed startled.

"Oh, yes." Vledder nodded with emphasis. "Their alibis were checked most thoroughly."

DeKok raised a finger in the air.

"But only for the murder of their *own* wife . . . or ex-wife."

The younger man gave him a pitying smile.

"Exactly, only for the murder of their own wives. Only in connection with their own respective spouses was there even a hint of a motive. It was senseless to check their movements in connection with the other women . . . women to whom they were not related in any way." Vledder paused briefly. "Headquarters, quite rightly, declined to do so," he added primly.

DeKok nodded vaguely, absent-mindedly. He found a piece of hard candy in his breast pocket, looked at it, unwrapped it and popped it in his mouth. Meanwhile his old brain worked at top speed, seemed to go into overdrive, soon galloped away with his imagination. It felt like he was floundering in a wild, uncontrolled maelstrom. A plan was taking shape, a fantastic plan, a plan so fantastic he could hardly credit himself with it.

"Do the men know each other?" he asked suddenly.

Vledder, who had been unable to follow DeKok's thoughts was understandably confused.

"The . . . eh, the men?" he asked, bewildered.

"Yes, the men, the husbands, or ex-husbands, of the victims," explained DeKok patiently. "Do they know each other? Was there any hint of contact between them . . . before, during, or . . . after the murders?"

Vledder made a helpless gesture.

"I don't know. As far as I know that was never checked." He shrugged his shoulders, dismissing the significance of the question. "Why would anybody want to check on *that*?"

"You see," answered DeKok pensively, "all eight of the men had a motive."

Vledder nodded reluctant agreement.

"Of course, but only in connection with their *own* wives. The usual thing, you know . . . tension between divorced people, disagreements about alimony, child support, visitation rights, education of the children." He gave a short, barking laugh without joy. "As a matter of fact, the victims don't show up all that well in the reports. They were all *greedy* women."

Deep in thought DeKok walked on. Then he stopped in the middle of the bridge just before Old Acquaintance Alley. He sagged a little and leaned his right hand on the bridge railing. He placed a confidential hand on his young colleague's shoulder.

"What if," he said carefully, "we pushed all the men up one notch?"

Vledder looked at him with a questioning expression.

"Push up one notch?"

"Yes," nodded DeKok. His face was serious. "For instance . . . divorced man 'a' kills the ex-wife of divorced man 'b' and divorced man 'b' kills the ex-wife of divorced man 'c' and so on, and so on . . ."

The young Inspector swallowed. His blue eyes were wide with wonder.

"You mean, the divorced men always kill the wife of the next one in line and thus kill the wife with whom they have no connection?" Vledder was wont to state the obvious. DeKok did not mind. It was the way the young Inspector placed the facts firmly in his mind. Vledder paused for a moment. "And for whom they have no motive?" he added.

DeKok leaned closer and placed a finger along the side of his nose.

"Excellent, really excellent," he praised. "And the divorced man who *does* have a connection with the victim *and* a motive for killing her, makes sure he has a perfect alibi." DeKok, too, was not averse to repeating the obvious when it suited him.

Vledder was flabbergasted. He looked at his old mentor with admiration.

"But that's *it*!" he exclaimed enthusiastically. "That's the solution. It's incredible ... just plain incredible." Another of Vledder's qualities was the ability to let enthusiasm run away with him. More often than not he had fastened on a particularly attractive theory and defended it against all comers. This time was no different. "No wonder," he went on, "that the guys from Headquarters never got anywhere. The way it's done there simply is no connection between the men and the victims. In order to discover that, you must be able to think around corners, the way you do."

DeKok leaned against the railing. His good-natured face was melancholy as he stared at the tips of his shoes. It was an idea, but there were a lot of unanswered questions, a lot of facets that needed to be explored, too many complications.

"It would require a monstrous agreement," he spoke out loud, "binding promises, and ..."

He did not complete the sentence. He stared upwards, far away, toward the domes and spires of the St. Nicholas Church. The church was named after the patron saint of sailors and the protector of children. When the Dutch went to the New World to found New Amsterdam, they brought their "Sinterklaas", as the saint is called in Dutch, with them. In America he eventually became known as Santa Claus. DeKok was lost in the sight of the beautiful church against the skyline and with a sigh he wondered, not for the first time, how so much beauty and good could co-exist in the same world with so much ugliness and evil. As always, when he looked at the church, he thought about happy children, but now the vision was blurred by an image of bloody sockets and crushed eyeballs.

"And what!?" urged Vledder

DeKok sighed deeply, came back to the present.

"And *shuto gammen-uschi*."

97

9

Inspector Vledder manoeuvred the police VW past a stream of cars behind the Royal Palace and into Town Hall Street. Much to DeKok's disgust he slipped through a yellow light and drove along Roses Canal.

The gray sleuth was slumped down in the passenger seat. DeKok did not care for traffic and even less for the automobiles that created the traffic. In his heart he longed for the time of the stage coach and the passenger barges that used to ply the many canals and rivers of the Netherlands. The passenger barge, pulled by one, or two horses, was in DeKok's opinion the most civilized mode of travel ever devised by man. Smoothly it would glide over the water, the passengers comfy and cozy in a large cabin, eating, drinking, smoking long, clay pipes. Pipes so fragile they invited calm and contemplation as the least little bump would break them. Ah, those were the days, he thought. None of this stop-and-go, loud noises and the pervasive stink of internal combustion engines.

At the end of Roses Canal Vledder turned off into Marnix Street and came to an abrupt stop in front of the Municipal Social Services building.

DeKok looked lazily at his young colleague.

"You're sure she's here?"

Vledder nodded, glancing at his watch.

"We made good time. I made an appointment for ten o'clock."

DeKok grunted. Vledder smiled. He knew DeKok would have preferred to walk. But sometimes the distances just weren't manageable in the available time.

They entered the somber building. People with bored faces leaned against the walls. There was a suffocating, tense atmosphere as if something was about to happen. The stillness before a storm, thought DeKok.

A woman approached them with decisive steps. DeKok estimated her to be in her early thirties. She wore solid walking shoes, a skirt that was just a little too long and a loose sweater, several sizes too large. She smiled broadly as she stretched out a strong hand toward the men.

"The gentlemen from the police." She sounded cheerful.

DeKok gave a her a winning smile.

"My name is DeKok . . ."

"With kay-oh-kay," added Vledder.

". . . and this is my colleague, Vledder," continued DeKok, ignoring the interruption.

She nodded her head in Vledder's direction.

"We spoke on the telephone, I believe?"

Vledder nodded shyly, overwhelmed by the robust vitality of the woman he had known only on the phone.

"Yes, Miss Graven, we did. If it's not too inconvenient, we'd like to elaborate a bit on that conversation."

She laughed at him with a playful look in her eyes.

"No need to be so formal. Just call me Catharine, or 'Cat'. That's what my mother called me. Miss Graven is much too much of a muchness," she joked.

She turned and led the way to a spacious office with a large desk. She waved toward a worn seating arrangement in one corner.

"What can I do for you?"

DeKok looked around. The decor of the room gave him the shivers. It was unsociable, indifferent, frostily institutionalized. Strictly business-like and without any frills. He could not discover a flower, or a plant. No pictures, no personal touches. Carefully he lowered himself into one of the old, rickety chairs.

"You . . . eh, you knew all the victims personally?"

Miss Graven sat down across from them. Ready and prepared. She crossed her skinny legs and pulled the skirt down over her knees. She nodded with emphasis. The cheer had left her face.

"Yes, I knew them. That's to say, in a professional capacity. As you may know, in the beginning of almost all divorce proceedings there are financial difficulties. The person left on his, or her own, can't cope. They are referred here and my department handles the inquiries."

DeKok nodded his understanding.

"That is before the courts have made their final decision?"

"Yes, during the legal separation stage, so to speak. In Holland we still use the quaint expression of being 'separated from table and bed'. In other words, the period before the divorce becomes final and many people, especially women, find themselves in a financial vacuum. We help bridge that time."

DeKok scratched the back of his neck.

"Apart from the fact that the women were divorced, or about to be divorced, did you find any similarities among the victims?"

Miss Graven seemed bored.

"The other policemen . . . the special unit? Headquarters? Yes, well, anyway, they asked me the same thing."

DeKok smiled reassuringly.

"And with reason, I should say. The mere fact that the women were divorced . . ." He held up a hand to forestall any objections. ". . . or about to be divorced," he continued, "could never, in itself, be a motive for murder. There must be tens of thousands of divorced women in our society."

Miss Graven seemed obtuse.

"You mean," she asked, as if it just became clear to her for the first time, "you mean that in addition to the divorced status, there must have been other factors?"

DeKok thought he had just explained that, but he answered patiently.

"Exactly. As of now nine women have been killed and we want to know what exactly determined the choice of the murderer."

Miss Graven looked pained.

"Of course, I'm entrusted with certain confidences, things that are said to me in confidence . . . in my professional capacity. Without revealing any secrets, I *can* tell you that the women, one and all, were not exactly the most *endearing* representatives of our sex. As a matter of fact, I can tell you unequivocally, rather the opposite."

DeKok's eyebrows rippled and Miss Graven actually leaned back in her chair, as if frightened by the sudden movement above the old cop's eyes. Vledder watched with interest. Miss Graven followed the same pattern as so many witnesses who had observed the phenomenon. Her eyes widened and then she blinked momentarily. Meanwhile the display had come to rest and when she looked again, she shook her head, blinked again. Then she realized that DeKok had asked a question.

"What did you say?" she asked, looking suspiciously at DeKok's forehead.

"Were they strong, unattractive women?" From experience DeKok knew that spousal abuse could be a two-way street.

Still wondering about what she had, or had not, seen, Miss Graven slowly shook her head.

"No . . . I didn't mean it that way. Nothing physical. Some were quite comely, as a matter of fact."

"Mental cruelty?"

DeKok sometimes liked to use the pseudo-psychological terms that seemed such a large part of official language. She stared at him, bit her lower lip and considered.

"In my profession," she said slowly, "I sometimes encounter situations that make me ashamed to be a woman."

"That bad?" asked DeKok, smiling gently.

She nodded to herself.

"Women are often so blunt, so . . . so, inhuman and freqently almost psychopathically selfish."

DeKok listened carefully to the bitter tone. It did not escape him that his use of a pseudo-psychological catch-phrase had elicited a similar response. He studied the face before him. After a long pause, he asked a question.

"You . . . eh, you," he began carefully, "you . . . don't like women?"

She shook her head vigorously.

"That would be a silly way to feel. Unnatural. After all, I'm a woman myself. But I detest women who degrade their husbands to the status of a slave, a serf . . . their subordinate. Women who see marriage solely as a sort of life insurance with the children as bond and as pawns." As she spoke her tone became sharper, louder. Blushes colored her cheeks. She obviously believed in what she was saying.

DeKok scratched the back of his neck. Slowly he rose from his chair.

"One of these days I'd like to discuss this in more detail," he said in a friendly tone of voice. He shook her hand and ambled in the direction of the door. Vledder followed close behind.

Near the door he turned, almost bumping into his young colleague. He walked back a few paces. His face was expressionless as he asked a last question.

"Miss Graven, do you practice karate?"

10

Vledder raced the engine of the old VW, switched gears roughly and savagely took his foot off the clutch pedal, depressing the gas pedal to the floor with his other foot. With loud protests and a banging exhaust, the old car pulled away from the curb. Vledder's face was red and there was a scowl on his face.

DeKok looked at him for some time, amused.

"Something bothering you?" he asked superfluously.

The young Inspector released some of the pressure on the gas pedal and cast a quick look in DeKok's direction.

"Whatever came over you to ask that woman if she practiced karate?" he asked, obviously irritated. "She was clearly upset."

DeKok looked his most guileless.

"But why should Miss Graven *not* practice karate?" he asked with well-feigned astonishment. "She seems to be the type of woman who might enjoy it."

Vledder pressed his lips together, swallowing an answer he might later regret.

"Well," he said with some delay, "you have your answer. Miss Graven does *not* practice karate. She didn't even know what you were talking about."

DeKok scratched the tip of his nose.

"Too bad," he sighed, "she would make such an ideal suspect."

That took Vledder by surprise.

"Miss Graven?" he asked, forgetting his irritation in favor of astonishment.

"Sure," answered DeKok calmly. "Just think. She knew almost all the victims personally . . . because of her job she knew all about their financial condition, their circumstances, their lifestyle . . . and she enjoyed their trust." The gray sleuth paused, looked out of the window without seeing anything. "In addition," he went on, "Miss Graven doesn't like divorced women, at least divorced women who shamelessly take advantage of their ex-husbands." He rubbed his chin and grinned without mirth. "I wouldn't be at all surprised if we found the works of Esther Vilar in her bookcase."

"Who's Esther Vilar?"

DeKok gave his partner a castigating look.

"You should read more," he chided. "Esther Vilar is a physician and author of *THE TRAINED MAN* and *THE POLYGAMIC SEX* . . . two books that created quite a furor, especially in Germany."

Vledder snorted.

"What does that have to do with the murders?"

"Maybe nothing," answered DeKok easily, "maybe everything. The biggest difficulty at this time is that any possible motive seems to be absent. Sure, no doubt we can find something in every *individual* case, but collectively there's no certain reason for murder, no clear motive." He suddenly slapped the dashboard. "Yet there *must* be an underlying reason for it all, a perceived motivation." He looked at Vledder. "Somewhere, somewhere in the twisted mind of that killer there has to be something that drives him."

Vledder shrugged his shoulders.

"All right, all right," he said, interested despite himself. "But what does it have to do with Esther Vilar?"

DeKok took a deep breath, settled himself a little more comfortably in the cramped seat of the old car.

"Esther Vilar attacks her own sex rather harshly. She takes the viewpoint that women have gradually trained men to be no more than decent, scared and hard-working providers for the women and children. She further states that the sexual reward doled out by women is hardly in proportion to the value received from men. And, she adds, in many cases the sexual act is reluctantly and unemotionally granted. It's more easily and above all, more cheaply, obtained from professionals. Because of this sexual depravation, this is still Esther talking, men are driven to find a polygamic solution. This instinct can be, of course, but seldom is satisfied because of a lack of proper finances. In short, without realizing it, the man has been reduced to no more than a slave, a serf of women." He grinned broadly. "And you'll remember that Miss Graven used similar words."

"So," commented Vledder, then asked: "What happens if the man realizes his condition?"

DeKok raked his fingers through his hair. His face showed a mild smile.

"Then he goes and visits Little Lowee."

Vledder laughed heartily.

"All right, you win. But that only applies to one man. But what have Esther Vilar's theories to do with Miss Graven?"

DeKok nodded to himself.

"Well, yes . . . that's a good question. But perhaps more importantly: What does Miss Graven *do* with Esther Vilar's theories?"

Vledder looked at him sharply, momentarily taking his eyes off the road.

"But she said she didn't know karate."

* * *

Another busy day at Sorrow Field. There were a lot of people to see Anna Henrietta Deel off to her last resting place. When the Chapel doors opened, they entered and took their seats facing the flower-bedecked coffin.

Vledder shook his head. His face was somber.

"If you don't mind, I won't come inside. All that ceremony always gives me a queasy feeling in my stomach. I'll wait for you in the car."

DeKok nodded permission.

"See you later."

He waved and was the last to enter the Chapel. Carefully he picked a place in the rear from which he had a good vantage point. He leaned against the wall and let his gaze wander among the visitors.

He discovered Charles Rozeblad in the first row. He was well groomed and wore a dark suit and a pearly-gray tie. He also seemed more self-assured, less tense than during the interview at Warmoes Street. Two children were seated beside him, a boy and a girl. They looked to be about four and six years old. They seemed uncomfortable in their black clothes and looked shyly at the crowd. Charles talked to them continually, softly, reassuringly and with loving attention. Every once in a while he placed a colossal hand on their heads, as if trying to protect them from evil.

DeKok remembered the karate lessons at VanLooijen's and wondered how much strength there was in the enormous hands and large body of Rozeblad. But strength had not been the deciding factor for the murder of the women. He had been sure to be informed on the subject. Jan VanLooijen had been explicit. The primary requirements for karate were speed and concentration.

Suddenly his thoughts ground to a halt. He had discovered a face on the other side of the coffin. A face that seemed vaguely familiar. He searched his memory, rifled feverishly for the small file cabinet in his brain that contained that particular memory.

Heavy organ music descended from the rafters and broke his concentration, just as he thought he had placed the familiar face. A few women to the right of him started to sob softly. Surreptitiously he moved sideways along the wall. If he could change his vantage point he could get a less obstructed view of the face.

Slowly he progressed. Some people looked at him, disturbed by his apparent lack of piety. Some people refused to move. DeKok was almost to the side wall when the organ music faded away and the pallbearers gathered around the coffin. The doors in the back walls opened without a sound and at an unseen command the pallbearers leaned toward the coffin and lifted it in an easy, effortless movement. Family members and other interested visitors sorted themselves out and slowly followed the retreating coffin.

DeKok was on the alert, ready to fasten his full attention on the face of the man he thought he recognized. Baffled and annoyed he discovered that the man seemed to have disappeared in thin air.

As soon as the building was completely empty and the back doors started to close to prepare for the next funeral, DeKok swiftly ran around the building and found Vledder in the old VW.

The young Inspector saw him approach with surprise.

"Finished already?"

The gray sleuth did not answer.

"Did you see anybody leave early, I mean, before they moved the coffin?" he asked hastily. "Or did you see a car suddenly leave?"

111

Vledder looked puzzled.

"I didn't particularly watch for that. There's people going in and out all the time."

"A man," explained DeKok, "about forty, just over six feet, sharp, lined face."

Vledder shrugged.

"I can't remember," he said nonchalantly and then, seeing DeKok's face, he added in a subdued voice: "Should I have?"

DeKok waved away the question. For several seconds he stared into the distance. He had the vague, uncomfortable feeling that he was missing something, something vital. It sent shivers down his spine and made his fingertips itch. Suddenly he turned around and ran back in the direction of the cemetery.

Despite the situation, Vledder could not help laughing. DeKok at speed was always a comical sight.

The gray cop panted heavily when he overtook the tail end of the procession. He forced his breathing into a calmer tempo as he meekly adjusted his pace to the more decorous speed of the pallbearers. Then he slowly worked his way forward through the crowd. He was already close to Charles Rozeblad and his two children when the coffin reached the grave site. The people formed a informal circle. The pallbearers placed the coffin on the grave lift and arranged the flowers.

Struck by a feeling of piety and respect, DeKok worked his way back to the outer edges of the circle. He ignored the angry looks from the people who's toes he had already stepped on in the Chapel. He looked on from a short distance. He had the overpowering feeling that he would see something, a clear observation in a matter of life and death.

His gaze became more restless as he studied the crowd. Out of the corner of his eyes he noticed Anna Deel's parents, two old, sorrowful people and a lump stuck in his throat. Through his own welling tears he cursed himself for a sentimental old fool. There were moments when he could be the cool, unemotional observer and then, such as now, his inner feelings would betray him and he was unable to see anything from blurred eyes because he allowed himself to be swept up in a stream of human suffering.

With considerable difficulty he overcame the lump in his throat and surreptitiously he wiped his eyes with the back of his hand. He tried to listen to the confused, teary voice of the father who spoke a last word at the grave. But the words were torn away by the slight breeze and only an infinitely heavy sense of loneliness and sorrow seemed to reach him.

Once again he looked around the circle of people surrounding the grave and suddenly he *knew* who was missing, who was not there, who should have been here. He was gripped by a fearful premonition. While Anna's father continued to murmur his unintelligible sorrow, he slinked away until he reached a side path and from there he ran back to the car.

Vledder was torn between amazement and amusement.

"Whatever are you doing?" he asked.

DeKok threw himself into the passenger seat.

"Do you have Josie Ardenwood's address?"

Vledder nodded and reached into an inside pocket for his notebook.

"Prince's Canal near Wester Market."

DeKok swallowed.

"Drive on, Dick, as fast as you can."

"Where?" asked Vledder as he threw the old vehicle into gear.

DeKok waved in the direction of the windshield.

"To Josie's . . . she wasn't at the funeral."

* * *

113

Vledder coaxed everything there was to be coaxed out of the old, decrepit vehicle and committed more traffic violations in nine minutes than the average citizen would normally commit in a lifetime. He slid sideways into position in front of the house on Prince's Canal. DeKok had left the car before it had come to a complete stop. He slammed the door behind him and ran, two, three steps at a time, up the narrow wooden stairs. There was a determined look in his face. He found a door ajar on the third floor. With his foot he pushed it wider. Carefully, prepared for any eventuality, he stepped inside, closely followed by Vledder.

* * *

They found Josie Ardenwood on the floor near the sofa. She was supine on the carpet and wore the same jean suit she had worn less than four days ago when the two cops had first met her in Anna Deel's house. Her legs were slightly spread and the arms were stretched out close to the body. The fingers, cramped, claw-like pointed at the ceiling.

DeKok knelt down next to her. The shadow of death had already marked her skin. He wiped a few strands of hair away from the mouth. The face was disfigured. Both eyeballs had been crushed and pushed out of the sockets. From the corners of the sockets thin trails of coagulated blood had formed a puddle in the ears. Dark red lumps of dried blood stuck to the blonde hair.

Slowly DeKok stood up. Suddenly he felt tired, worn out with a fatigue that was mental as well as physical. He looked his age.

Vledder came to stand next to him. The young man's face still wore the traces of the hair-raising trip through the city. He wiped his mouth with the back of his hand.

"We're too late," he said tonelessly.

DeKok nodded slowly, too weary for words.

After a long pause, he finally spoke three words.

"Alert the *Herd*."

11

Dr. Koning looked closely at the corpse. He felt the lower jaw, both legs and placed the back of his hands against the dead cheek. Slowly he rose from his squatting position. DeKok hastened to help the old man.

"Rigor mortis is general," said the Coroner.

"And what does that mean?" asked DeKok.

"That she has been dead between eight and twelve hours."

"Could you be more precise?" grimaced DeKok.

The old Coroner made a helpless gesture.

"It will have to do."

"The thermometer?"*

"Useless. She's been dead too long."

DeKok looked pensively at the doctor. The old man was more loquacious than usual. Everybody seemed to go out of their way to help him with this case. Dr. Koning had already confirmed the cause of death without being urged. Normally he would either refuse such information, or express himself in the most guarded terms.

"Eight to twelve hours," DeKok thought out loud. "That means she was killed late last night, or early in the morning." He

---

* To determine the time of death with the so-called corpse thermometer, based on the fact that the body temperature of a corpse drops approximately 1 Centigrade per hour.

117

turned toward Vledder. "Has the bed been slept in?"

"No."

"Signs of a break-in?"

"No, everything is untouched. She must have opened the door for the murderer."

"How's that?"

Vledder pointed.

"There's a small window in the door and there's a light over the door. The outside light is in working order . . . I tried. Thus she was able to see her visitor clearly and let him enter. The chain has been removed in the normal way, no sign of force."

"Did she normally use the chain."

"Yes, according to the neighbors. Even during the day. Josie Ardenwood was a 'scaredy-cat' according to one neighbor. She kept all strangers outside her door."

"So, the murderer wasn't a stranger, eh?"

"Not to her," agreed Vledder. "In any case, she trusted her visitor enough to remove the chain from the door." His face fell. "Her trust became her death."

DeKok nodded to himself and looked around the room . . . the pretentious sofa arrangement, the table with a heavy onyx top and the heavy, expensive carpet with the same luxurious flower motif as that of Anna Deel. He saw the telephone, discreetly hidden in a small cabinet, now open, near the window.

"Perhaps the murderer made an appointment and she expected him."

Dr. Koning tapped his shoulder.

"I'm leaving," said the eccentric old man. "I'll see you at the next one." He sounded discouraged.

Weelen, the photographer, came closer and eyed DeKok with a pitying smile.

"You see what I mean?" he asked angrily. "That's how it goes. They're leaving it all to you. Believe me, those guys at

Headquarters are laughing at your expense. They're just waiting for you to fall on your face."

"Why would that be funny?" asked DeKok.

The photographer shook his head in despair.

"Don't you see? It was a rotten trick to stick you with this case in the first place. Every new killing damages your reputation while they're safe, unconcerned. You're the fall-guy."

DeKok pressed his lips together and for just a moment he looked angry. Then he realized that Weelen was truly concerned and he relented.

"I don't care about my reputation," he said easily. "Whatever that may be. And if anybody thinks this is some sort of game, a race between Headquarters and me, well . . . I don't get involved in that sort of comparison."

"Besides," piped up Vledder, "we didn't get the case until eight people had already been killed." He gestured toward the corpse in the floor. "This is only our second murder on our fourth day. We're way ahead of the competition."

DeKok placed a calming hand on the shoulder of his assistant and gave him a disapproving look. Weelen shrugged his shoulders and disappeared.

The two morgue attendants came closer, placed the body on the stretcher and carried it away.

Kruger packed his paraphernalia. DeKok addressed him.

"I haven't heard a thing from you, yet," he chided.

The fingerprint expert looked up.

"About the last one?"

"Of course."

Kruger made an apologetic gesture.

"I'm working on it. You'll get a complete rundown on all the prints we found. I'm almost finished with it. There was nothing there, nothing important, I mean. Otherwise I would have called you at once." He searched in his case and pulled out a folder that contained a number of silvery fingerprints on a black material. "The only repeat was that lawyer." He looked through the folder. "I bet he's here as well."

DeKok's eyes flashed.

"Lawyer?"

"Oh, yes, I've encountered his fingers at least four times."

"In this series of murders?"

"Indeed," smiled Kruger shyly. "Yes, in this series of murders. But don't get your hopes up. It's nothing. The man has been interrogated extensively by Headquarters."

DeKok was getting excited.

"Four times?" he exclaimed. "The same guy?"

Kruger nodded.

"Maybe more often. I'll look it up for you, if you wish."

DeKok snorted, his nostrils widened and his face clouded over.

"What did he want with all these women?" he asked loudly, demandingly.

Vledder intervened hastily.

"He was their divorce lawyer," he explained hurriedly. "If you had read the files, you would have known."

Kruger looked at DeKok for several seconds. Then he closed his case and left without greeting.

DeKok watched him go with mixed emotions. When the door closed behind the specialist, DeKok turned toward Vledder.

"What's the name of that guy?"

"Kruger? Oh, yes, sorry, you mean the lawyer?"

"Yes."

Vledder grinned maliciously.

"E.G. Hareberg, Esquire. He resides, as they say, at Emperor's Canal."

* * *

Vledder found a parking meter near the water's edge. They got out of the car and quickly crossed the road. They climbed the steps toward the front door and stopped on the wide stoop. A large, dark-green door confronted them. A sign next to the door announced: *E.G. Hareberg, Attorney-at-Law* with deeply engraved, black letters on a copper plate. DeKok pushed against the door and, followed by Vledder, entered a long, marble corridor.

A man came out of a door off to the side. He looked to be about thirty years old, with a sallow face and flaxen hair parted with a precise part on the side. Of medium height, with round shoulders and arms that seemed too long, he gave a dull, almost retarded impression. Slowly, hesitatingly he shuffled closer.

DeKok made a slight bow.

"We're here to see Mr. Hareberg."

The man looked intently at the two cops from behind thick glasses in a round, steel frame.

"You have an appointment?" His voice sounded creaky, as if he was twice his apparent age.

DeKok nodded calmly.

"Yes, with the Netherlands government, if you must know."

A modest smile curled around the man's lips.

"I mean, do you have an appointment with Mr. Hareberg?"

The gray sleuth shook his head.

"No, but I'm sure he'll see us. My name is DeKok . . . with . . . eh, kay-oh-kay." He pointed at Vledder. "This is my partner, Vledder. We are police detectives."

The man smiled thinly.

"I thought so. One moment, please."

He disappeared through the same door from which he had emerged. After a few minutes he came back and led the visitors to a high-ceilinged, large room.

A good-looking man in his fifties stepped around an enormous desk and approached them with a youthful step. He shook hands with such strength that Vledder winced momentarily.

"A surprise," the man called out in a cheerful voice. "I would never, ever, have expected to be honored by a visit from the famous DeKok himself. To meet you, and your partner in person . . . wonderful, wonderful. And in my own office, of all places."

DeKok looked impassively. Then his gaze wandered to the lighthearted, almost indecently sensual, naked cherubims that had been modeled on the ceiling.

Mr. Hareberg continued happily.

"How can I be of service to you, gentlemen?" With a big hand he pointed at some large, comfortable, leather chairs. "But, please, sit down. A sherry?" "He laughed too heartily, with too much gold flickering among his white teeth. "No, of course not, it's cognac, isn't it?"

DeKok seated himself. His face remained expressionless.

"I've come to inform you about the death of Josephine Ardenwood," he said bitterly. He looked evenly at the jolly lawyer. "Or is that superfluous information?"

The lawyer's face paled.

"Josie . . . Josie Ardenwood is dead?" he lisped.

DeKok nodded.

"We found her less than an hour ago, dead in her house," he said, hard, implacable. "Murdered in the same way as the nine others."

Hareberg hid his face in his hands.

DeKok reacted unusually venomously.

"Take your hands away," he ordered, "I want to see your face."

The lawyer lowered his hands, a watchful look in his eyes.

"What gives you the right to use that tone of voice with me?" he asked, taken aback.

"Ten murdered women, Mr. Hareberg, don't allow me time for politeness."

Hareberg nodded to himself, then shook his head.

"I have nothing to do with those murders. I have explained that in some detail to your colleagues from Headquarters ... your superiors? The only relationship between me and those women is that I acted as their counsel during the divorce proceedings."

"That's all?"

Hareberg was getting irritated.

"What are you implying?"

DeKok leaned forward.

"Perhaps there was more ... more than just a *professional* relationship with the victims."

Hareberg swallowed.

"I'm sorry ... I don't understand."

DeKok grinned wickedly. There was none of the boyish charm that usually lit up his face when he grinned for joy. When DeKok grinned that way he was irresistible. But the way he grinned this time seemed to make him more frightening.

"Is it usual," asked DeKok, "for a divorce lawyer to visit his female clients in their homes?"

Hareberg seemed unsure of himself. He shrugged his shoulders, spread his hands and blinked several times.

"No, not usual, no ... but there are circumstances, I mean, in certain cases ..."

DeKok waved away the remarks.

"You deliberately cultivated relations with these women . . . intimate relationships."

"No," denied the lawyer, "that's pertinently not true. I contest that and I object to your insinuation."

DeKok smiled sarcastically.

"We're not in court, besides . . . I wouldn't advise that sort of defense if I were you." He made an expansive gesture. "One should never deny the facts, incontrovertible facts."

Hareberg reacted in a confused manner.

"What sort of incontrovertible facts . . . what are you talking about?"

DeKok wiggled his fingers at the lawyer.

"Your fingerprints, Mr. Hareberg, your fingerprints were found in the houses of the women who were killed,"

The lawyer managed a sweet-and-sour smile.

"I have adequately explained that."

DeKok laughed heartily, mocking the man with his manner and his tone.

"What sort of explanations? The ridiculous story that you visited those women in your capacity as counsel?" He snorted. "We found your fingerprints in the bedrooms of the murdered women. What were you doing there? Did you dispense judicial advice in bed?" DeKok's voice dripped with sarcasm. "You had relationships with those women," he went on, "sexual relationships."

"No, no," protested the lawyer in a weak voice.

DeKok came out of his easy chair and with loud, heavy steps approached the desk. He banged his fist on the surface.

"Here," he yelled, "here at this desk. At this desk you sorted them out, you made your selections, you chose the women who might just qualify for the attentions of E.G. Hareberg, *Esquire*." He practically spat out the honorific and walked back in the direction of the lawyer. He stopped in front of the man and looked down at him. "And they were quite willing, weren't they? The great and famous Mr. Hareberg, the celebrated lawyer . . . who would be able to resist your charms?"

"No, no," repeated the lawyer softly. His eyes darted around the room, trying to avoid the cruel grin and the devilish gleam in DeKok's eyes.

"Of course," persisted DeKok in a low, threatening voice, "The relationships could never be of a permanent nature, not even for an extended period of time, could they? There could be no time for love, or affection to develop. That would be too bothersome and the women might just be a threat to the reputation of the incorruptible and *honorable* Mr. Hareberg, the *respected* husband, *esteemed* pillar of the community and father of three college-age children."

DeKok reseated himself.

"Mr. Hareberg," he said evenly, "it's confession time."

12

DeKok had tired feet. A small army of hellish needle wielders marched agonizingly from his ankles to his calves and tortured the flesh as they went. He knew that pain. It was a bad sign, as he also knew. It happened almost every time when his investigations had reached a nadir, when he became discouraged and was overpowered by the feeling that the solution would never be found. It was purely psychosomatic, he had been assured, but was nevertheless very real for all that.

With a painful grimace he lifted his feet and carefully, gingerly, placed them on top of his desk. He released a deep sigh, mostly because the manoeuvre had been successfully completed.

Vledder pushed a chair closer to his desk. His face looked concerned, because he knew all about the symptoms and also what they meant. But he could not altogether suppress a smile as he looked at his old partner.

"You really gave Mr. Hareberg a piece of your mind. For a moment I really thought he would confess to the murders."

The gray sleuth shook his head.

"It was no good, no good at all, at all. I was just in a bad mood. Josie's corpse set me off, I guess. I ruined the interview. I behaved like a bull in a china shop."

Vledder laughed out loud.

"You can say that again. The pieces flew around his ears. I've seldom seen anybody have the wind taken out of his sails faster and more thoroughly in less time."

DeKok smiled wanly, still racked by pain.

"In a way I was right, though. Mr. Hareberg had a relationship with more than one of the women."

"Yes," nodded Vledder, "But not with all of them. He was careful to select the best looking clients."

"And that," admitted DeKok, "makes him less of a suspect . . . unfortunately."

"But why?" wondered Vledder. "He did *know* them all. And he was a man who enjoyed the complete trust of the victims . . . they would open their doors for him anytime."

"That's exactly the crux of the matter," answered DeKok slowly. "Somehow, despite all that, he doesn't fit the overall pattern of the murders. And that's a prime requirement, you'll agree. We can't afford the luxury of sub-dividing the ten murders in groups. No four-four-two, or three-three-four, or anything like that. Based on the *modus operandi*, all murders were committed by the same person."

"Yes, but . . ." interrupted Vledder.

"Mr. Hareberg," continued DeKok, waving away the interruption, "had a relationship with four of the ten women. If, by some chance, those relationships created a motive, he would *only* have killed those four. The others just don't signify in that scenario. And another thing," he added, "I took a good look at his hands. I don't think that Mr. Hareberg ever had anything to do with karate."

Vledder nodded pensively.

"Maybe you're right. Maybe he isn't our man. After all, Mr. Hareberg had a number of relationships with women who are still very much alive."

"How did you find that out?" DeKok was astonished.

"Well," smiled Vledder, "there was *something* about your accusations. Afterward I called around and did some research on the respected counselor. He's known far and wide as a *bon-vivant*, a hedonist, who breaks off liaisons as easily as he commits to them." He held up a finger. "Did you know he also does work for Tropic Oil?"

DeKok lifted his feet off the desk and turned to look Vledder full in the face.

"Tropic Oil?"

"Yes, he's friends with Gellecom . . . and now that I think about it . . . he was also at Dinterloo's funeral."

DeKok looked interested. Then he started to search his pockets. Vledder waited patiently until DeKok eventually found a forgotten stick of chewing gum, slowly unwrapped it and started to chew. His face reposed into thoughtful silence.

"The naked lady," he whispered after a long pause. For another moment he remained deep in thought. Then, as if throwing off a burden, he stood up, went to the coat rack and grabbed his hat and coat. "Come on," he called cheerfully, "let's hit the road."

"Where to?"

"To a house on a lake, north of the city," he said mysteriously.

"And what are we looking for?"

DeKok was already in motion toward the door.

"A woman," he called over his shoulder.

Vledder hastened to catch up.

"A woman?" he asked, as they descended the stairs.

"Yes," answered DeKok. A woman who has known for months, maybe years, all there is to know about *shuto gammen-uschi*."

* * *

129

They took the Harbor Tunnel and emerged north of the city. Vledder drove, of course. DeKok watched him and wondered how the young man was able to smoothly change gears without grinding. The only sound was the occasional misfire of the engine, the constant rattling of the old vehicle and the rushing of the slip-stream. Once out of the tunnel, Vledder aimed for Purmerend. Near the soccer field at Ilpendam he slowed down and parked on the shoulder. He pointed at the canal.

"Hereabouts is where Dinterloo drove into the canal and drowned," he said.

DeKok looked at the bushes that screened the sight of the canal.

"He came from the opposite side."

"There, near the bend," said Vledder, "that's where he must have lost control."

"Strange," observed DeKok, scratching the tip of his nose. "You can hardly call it a bend in the road. It's more a very gradual veering of direction."

"Maybe it's true," shrugged Vledder. "Maybe he was blinded by traffic from the other direction." He moved the gears, glanced in the side mirror and pulled away. "You have to remember . . . it was a dark night."

DeKok did not bother to answer. He squirmed a bit lower in the seat and pulled his little old hat deeper into his eyes. They had driven several miles before he spoke again.

"How far until we get there?" he asked suddenly.

"Maybe another twenty-five kilometers."

"About twenty, maybe thirty minutes?"

"Just about."

"Have you ever heard of a drug, or anesthetic that becomes active after half an hour, maybe forty-five minutes?"

Vledder was confused and momentarily took his eyes off the road.

"You think that Dinterloo . . ."

DeKok shook his head, pursed his lips.

"No, I was just thinking of the possibility."

* * *

Rijp turned out to be a friendly little town, almost unchanged since the Middle Ages. The Town Hall looked like something from a fairy tale. The few new constructions surrounding it formed a harsh contrast to the soft lines and weathered bricks of the older buildings. They passed through the town and asked an old woman, dressed in traditional garb, for directions to Globdike Street. The old woman laughed with a mouth devoid of teeth and pointed to a large house shaped like a Swiss chalet. There, she assured the men, they would find the Gellecoms.

About a hundred feet before they reached the villa, Vledder parked the car in a convenient spot. They left the car and proceeded on foot. The chalet was surrounded by a magnificent garden. Conifers formed restful counterpoints of ocher, green and purple in a colorful sea of flowers. In addition to a footpath leading to the imposing front door, there was a driveway leading to a number of garages. A large Rolls Royce was parked in front of one of the garage doors. DeKok recognized the car. When they approached they saw an older man, dressed in a yellow duster, polishing the enormous hood of the magnificent automobile. The man looked up. A happy smile lit up his face.

"I've seen you two before," he said.

"That's right," agreed DeKok. "In Amsterdam. Sorrow Fields. At the funeral of Professor Dinterloo."

The man nodded seriously.

"I remember," he said pensively. "I was waiting there." He looked at DeKok and then at Vledder. "But why are you here?" he asked, surprise in his voice.

131

DeKok looked around.

"We came to admire the garden," he evaded. "It's truly a treasure."

The man put away his polishing cloth and leaned against the front door of the car. He felt in the pocket of his duster and found a pack of cigarettes. He offered the pack to the cops, but they politely declined. With precise, economic movements the man lit a cigarette for himself.

"It's all the work of Madame," he explained. "The garden is her hobby . . . her love, you might say. She really has a green thumb, you know. It's unbelievable . . . the results she can get from trees and flowers, anything that grows. She even manages to grow crocuses in the fall."

The gray sleuth smiled politely.

"Doesn't mean a thing to me," he said cheerfully "For the last quarter century or more, I've been confined to Amsterdam and the only kind of Madams we have there are only interested in raising other things."

The man looked momentarily confused.

"Madams?" he asked. Then he understood the allusion and smiled faintly. But DeKok paid no attention.

"I mean, what does the average Amsterdammer know about nature? About flora and fauna? Maybe, if he's lucky, he'll go to the Zoo, once or twice in his life." He grinned. "An Amsterdammer knows only two kind of birds: finches and floating finches."

"Floating finches?"

"Ducks and swans," explained DeKok. "In Amsterdam," he lectured on, "if it's green it's either a tree, a bush, or grass. Height determines the classification. A bird is a finch and if it lives on the water, we call it a floating finch. Anything with color is a flower . . . just a flower, no particular kind." He paused. "Sad, really," he added.

132

The man was slightly overwhelmed by DeKok's diatribe. It took a while before he again trusted himself to speak.

"But," he said after a while, "I don't think you came here for the garden."

"You're right," smiled DeKok and lifted his hat politely. "My name is DeKok and this is my partner Vledder. We're cops, assigned to the renowned station in Warmoes Street."

The man looked amazed.

"Inspectors? Has something happened to the Master . . . to Madame?"

"They're not home?"

The man pointed at the car.

"The Master is on a business trip to the United States. Madame has gone shopping and took the Jaguar."

"Is she going to be long?"

The man shrugged.

"I don't think so. As a matter of fact, I expect her back any moment." He looked at DeKok. "You intend to wait for her?"

"Absolutely."

"In that case," said the man, after some reflection, "I'll have you taken to the salon." He leaned inside the car window and pressed the horn. In response to the sound a woman appeared a few minutes later. She was about forty, estimated DeKok. She wore heavy, shapeless shoes, a severe black skirt and a white, silk blouse, buttoned to the top.

"Mrs. Vries," said the man formally, "these gentlemen are from the police. They are here to see Madame."

Mrs. Vries gave the two men an arrogant, deprecating look from her dark-green eyes. Silently she led the way. Through the garage they reached an impressive foyer and from there she led them through a wide corridor to a sunny room with a magnificent view of the gardens.

"A jolly old thing," murmured Vledder when they were left alone.

DeKok did not respond. With his hat in one hand he looked around. The room was expensively furnished in the modern style. The gray sleuth discovered a fortune in paintings on the walls ... impressionists, Renoir, Monet, Pissarro, Cezanne. They looked authentic.

They heard the growling of a powerful engine outside. It took a while, but then she entered: a mesmerizing woman. She dropped a stack of parcels on a sofa and with a bright look in her eyes she approached the two men.

"What a surprise," she laughed. "So unexpected, the famous detecting duo in my own house." She made a graceful gesture in the direction of some stylish, white chairs. "Can I count on your undivided attention?" She threw her head back and gave a challenging laugh. "It would be a real pleasure."

DeKok looked at her without any expression on his face.

"Mrs. Gellecom," he said in a steely voice, "you may indeed be assured of our undivided attention." He paused for effect. "But I can't promise you that it will be a pleasure, for either of us."

She sat down across from the Inspectors. Her attitude was frivolous, nonchalant and seductive.

"Oh, come, come," she waved, "for what crime am I under suspicion?"

DeKok merely looked at her.

"Murder," he said flatly.

Diana Gellecom seemed momentarily affected. A shadow flashed across her face, but she quickly recovered.

"Surely you're not serious."

DeKok gave her a winning smile.

"Murder," he said in a friendly tone of voice, "is often closer to home than we think."

She shook her head, indicating the garden.

"You're a somber man, Mr. DeKok. Look outside, look at the garden. Such light, such sun, what colors. Who can think of murder when looking at it?"

"Me," said DeKok stubbornly. He pushed his lower lip forward. There was a hint of a bulldog in his features.

Diana shrugged her shoulders in a helpless gesture.

"You . . . you're incorrigible." It sounded like an accusation.

DeKok scratched the back of his neck.

"You object to frankness?"

She seemed unsure of herself.

"No, no," she said, shaking her head. "Not at all." It did not sound very convincing.

DeKok smiled and leaned closer.

"How much, Mrs. Gellecom, did you love Fred Dinterloo?"

She jumped up as if stung by a bee. Her eyes flashed. For the first time she lost her pose, showed her true self: A temperamental young woman very much aware of her rights and privileges.

"That is an impertinent . . . an indecent question to ask a married woman," she exclaimed passionately.

DeKok spread his arms as if to emphasize his innocence.

"You did give me permission," he justified.

Diana sat down again. The frivolous impression had completely disappeared. She seemed calmer, more intent.

"I loved Fred," she said softly. "More than I realized while he was still alive."

DeKok looked at her searchingly.

"You only fully realized that *after* he was dead?"

She stared into the distance, pensively, without answering.

"Well?" urged DeKok.

"I'm a modern woman," she said finally, softly. "For me marriage doesn't have the same implications, the same values as is commonly understood. I interpret the wedding vows more liberally. When I got to know Max Gellecom he *seemed* the ideal man. He was big and important, rich, impressive and very sure of himself . . . without weaknesses. Calculatingly, but also because of admiration, I married him."

Vledder made an unintelligible sound and DeKok shot him a warning look. Diana Gellecom continued, did not take notice of the sound, or the glance.

"Later, much later, I discovered that his importance, his inaccessibility was caused by an amazing lack of capacity for love, an absence of any humane feelings. He's no more than a computer, a calculating machine in the shape of a human. A man without feelings, without sentiment. I've been unfaithful to him from the moment I made that discovery. I looked for and found fleeting contacts with other men. Not on the sly, not secretively, but openly. It didn't mean a thing. It was no more than a challenge, a taunting of Max." She smiled bitterly. "He allowed it all . . . wasn't even able to bring up enough emotion to be jealous, or angry, mentally incapable to feel the challenge."

DeKok raked his fingers through his hair.

"So, your relationship with Dinterloo was no more than a taunting of your husband?"

She shook her head in sadness.

"No, despite my reputation, despite all the previous adventures, there never was any relationship between Fred and me. It was love. I was truly and honestly in love, without any ulterior motives. Fred was so different. The things I originally admired in Max, were totally lacking in Fred. On the contrary, he was unsure of himself, confused and despite his high intelligence . . . no more than a helpless child. It was quite an experience to

136

meet him, a total shock and such a relief. He was so, so . . . *different*. I fell in love, a feeling I had never had before."

"And you asked Fred to get a divorce?"

She reacted strongly.

"Of course . . . I wanted to marry him."

DeKok gestured around, encompassing the garden, the paintings, the luxurious surroundings.

"And give up all this?"

"I . . . eh, Max and I, we had an agreement." There was a wary look in her eyes.

DeKok pressed his lips together. For a moment he said nothing, allowed her last words to hang in the air. Then he spoke.

"You knew and *know* very well that Max Gellecom would resist any attempt at divorce. He would never agree. His untouchable, calculating computer soul would resist any such attempts."

She reacted furiously. Her nostrils quivered.

"I would have found a way."

DeKok nodded slowly, the beginning of a crooked grin around his mouth.

"Murder," he said contemptuously.

He rose from the easy chair and stood in front of her . . . broad, large and threatening.

"Diana Gellecom, who is the Naked Lady?"

She looked at him with an expression of confused fear. The color drained from her face. Then she collapsed.

13

DeKok looked down on the collapsed woman in the chair. He looked at her shoulders, the arms, the right hand which was flat in her lap. The gray sleuth wondered if he had been too harsh, if he had toyed too much with her emotions. There were people who could stand but few emotions. He motioned toward Vledder.

"Find that Mrs. Vries. She'll be around here somewhere."

The young Inspector nodded and left the room. He was back after a few minutes, accompanied by Mrs. Vries. She leaned over the unconscious Diana Gellecom. Then she looked up, hate and disgust in her eyes.

"What did you do to her?" she wailed. Her high voice shrieked painfully.

DeKok shook his head, outwardly unperturbed.

"Perhaps you could fetch some *eau de cologne*, or some *sale volatile*. Madame seems to have suffered a slight collapse."

Mrs. Vries confronted him in a threatening manner.

"I will complain about you. She has friends in the highest circles." She waved a hand in the air. "You . . . you . . . you with your, with your *Amsterdam* methods!"

DeKok took her by the arm and pushed her out of the room.

"Do as you're told," he growled brusquely.

139

He closed the door behind her and went back to the unconscious woman. He lifted her eyelids with a careful finger and softly, almost tenderly, he tapped her cheeks. After a few seconds she opened her eyes and looked at him.

"W-wha . . . what happened?" she asked faintly.

DeKok nodded encouragingly.

"You . . . eh, you were gone there, for a while," he soothed.

Mrs. Vries stormed back into the room. She stopped in front of Mrs. Gellecom and looked at her in amazement.

"I . . . I . . . but I called the doctor."

Mrs. Gellecom made a repudiating gesture.

"Call him back," she ordered. "Tell him he's not needed. It was a mistake."

DeKok smiled quietly at the regained strength in her voice.

* * *

They drove along the dike between the Beemster and Purmer polders on the way back to Amsterdam. Comfortably sagged in the seat, DeKok looked at the wide, flat landscape and the pale blue sky with a tolerant eye. This was the oldest as well as the newest part of Holland. He reflected that only a Dutchman would understand the contradiction. But in this area, Holland's battle with the sea had begun. Nearby was one of DeKok's fishing holes and this area was one of his favorite places in Holland.

Purmerend, vaguely visible in the distance, is famous in Holland for a number of reasons. It is situated between the former Beemster and Purmer lakes. These two lakes are part of the first five lakes drained by the legendary Jan Adriaenz Leeghwater and formed a decisive turning point in Holland's continual battle against the sea. The Purmer was also the first lake to be drained entirely by windmills with a movable cap, to which the wings were attached, and an outside winding gear.

Until that time mills had a fixed cap, requiring them to be stopped when the wind changed, then turning the entire structure into the wind before pumping could be resumed. The new mills allowed for wind changes without having to interrupt the vital pumping process. The work on the Purmer was completed in 1631 and yielded more than 12,000 acres of new land. Work on the five lakes commenced in 1597 with the construction of dikes around the lakes and almost 200 windmills were specifically built for the project to pump the water into the surrounding canals and from there to the sea. Altogether Leeghwater created more than 250,000 acres for the Netherlands in his lifetime and laid the foundation for later, more ambitious projects. The surface of the former lakes, called "polders", is an average of twelve feet below see level, only protected by sand dunes and the 17th Century dikes.

"Let's say you're married," said DeKok suddenly. "Would you give up a life of luxury just because you didn't like your spouse?" His face looked thoughtful, as if he was answering himself.

"I hope you don't mind my saying so, DeKok," groused Vledder, "but you're a strange person at times."

"Why do you say that?" asked DeKok, genuinely amazed.

Vledder banged the steering wheel with one hand,

"Like now for instance," he protested. "First we drive all the way to Rijp, past Rijp, to ask Mrs. Gellecom about *shuto gammen-uschi* and when we get there you don't breathe a word about karate."

DeKok unearthed a roll of peppermints in the glove compartment. With a happy sigh he popped one in his mouth and offered the roll to Vledder. The young man glanced aside and refused with a curt shake of his head.

"You're right," conceded DeKok, picking up the conversation, "I planned to do so, but the interview just went off on a tangent. But I did notice her hands and I'm of the opinion . . . an uninformed opinion, no doubt . . . but I'm of the opinion that the metacarpal bones, the edge of her right hand seemed more developed than the other. Perhaps we can ask Jan VanLooijen what she's capable of."

"If you ask me," leered Vledder, "she's capable of quite a lot, physically that is."

DeKok nodded to himself.

"An enchanting woman," he said pensively. "And my question about the naked lady had definite results."

"She fainted."

"An easy way out. A typically feminine tactic."

"You sound like a chauvinist, you know that?"

"Yes, I'm sorry, but you will agree that men usually don't faint under the same circumstances. Sometimes it makes me mad."

"But why?"

"It's a fact that women, on the average, are physiologically much stronger than men. But yet, some women faint at the drop of a hat. All theatrics."

Vledder could not let that go. DeKok, of all people, was accusing someone of theatrics. In Vledder's opinion DeKok was often guilty of theatrics. It always amazed the young Inspector that people did not see through his old partner at once. But they never did. This time, however, thought Vledder, it's clearly a case of the pot and the kettle.

"Why shouldn't women faint," he objected. "If a person is sensitive enough . . ."

"Spare me," growled DeKok. "My old mother used to say something about that. *If women and men had to have children in turn*, she used to say, *there would never be a family with more than three children*. No," he added decisively, "women are tougher than men."

Vledder decided not to pursue the subject.

"You think she knows the Naked Lady?"

"Yes, she does," answered DeKok.

"She does?" Vledder was dumbfounded.

DeKok pushed his hat further back on his head.

"I gave the driver our phone number. He's to call us immediately if something happens to Gellecom."

"Her husband?"

"Yes, the Tropic Oil CEO is in great danger."

* * *

"Eh . . . aren't . . . I mean you're responsible for the murders of those women, aren't you?"

DeKok looked up from some papers Vledder had handed him. Fred Prins, one of the newer Inspectors assigned to Warmoes Street station, stood in front of his desk. There was an anxious look on his honest, open face.

"No, I'm not," said DeKok.

"But I thought . . . they said . . ."

"I know what you mean," interrupted DeKok, "but I'm not responsible for the murders. I have been placed in charge of the *investigations* concerning the murders."

Prins sighed with relief and smiled happily.

"Sorry, yes, that's exactly what I mean."

"Well, now that we have cleared that up, what can I do for you?" asked DeKok, pointing at the chair next to his desk.

Prins sat down.

"I heard about it," he said, "they really stuck it to you, didn't they?"

DeKok grinned self-consciously.

"Yes, that seems to be the general opinion and I'm inclined to agree with it." He looked at the young, eager policeman and pushed the papers in a drawer. "But surely," he continued, "you have more on your mind than to express your sympathy?"

Fred Prins nodded agreement and pushed his chair closer to the desk.

"I want to talk to you. You see, I read an article that started me thinking."

"What sort of article?"

Prins handed DeKok a newspaper.

"The article is in there. It's an interview with a man who has been paying a hefty alimony for more than twenty-five years to a woman to whom he was married for less that three years. He's been in and out of the courts in order to get relief from the alimony, but every time he lost."

"And?" asked DeKok tensely.

"Vledder told me that all the women were divorced and receiving alimony."

"That's about right, yes."

Fred raked a hand through his hair in a subconscious imitation of one of DeKok's gestures.

"Well, the man said something in that interview that struck me as significant. 'For a murder they give you a few years, but for a failed marriage you get a life sentence,' he said."

DeKok looked thoughtful.

"Meaning of course," he commented superfluously, "that it's cheaper to kill your wife than to divorce her."

"Exactly," said Prins. "An excellent motive, don't you think?"

DeKok smiled a friendly smile.

"And what's the name of the man from the interview?"

Fred Prins, like a good cop, consulted his notebook while pointing at the newspaper. "A Mr. Winepresser. I looked up his address. It's 93 Heart Street, second floor."

DeKok stood up.

"Where's Vledder?"

"Downstairs, or next door. He wanted some *good* coffee, he said."

"Call him," ordered DeKok. Then he hesitated, took a second look at the eager young face. "Never mind. Get your coat. It was your idea, after all."

The younger man smiled proudly.

"Where are we going?"

"To see Mr. Winepresser, of course. I want to know who his friends are."

* * *

"What kind of friends?" Mr. Winepresser shook his head. "I don't have many true friends. I do have acquaintances and some sympathizers, men who, like me committed a horrible crime . . . they married the wrong woman."

"Surely, that's no crime," grinned DeKok.

"Of course," gestured Winepresser, "I was totally unaware that a crime had been committed. No man goes to Town Hall with the knowledge that he's marrying the wrong woman. But, if later it comes about that he *did* make the wrong choice, his punishment will be worse than if he were a murderer. He gets a life sentence."

"I'm familiar with the arguments you presented in your interview," nodded DeKok. "You also stated that it would be cheaper to simply kill the ex-wife."

Mr. Winepresser looked sad.

"It's the logical consequence of our distorted system of justice. Divorce is usually loaded with emotions. Both parties make the foulest accusations and the bitterest charges. They blame each other for the failure of the marriage. I can understand all that, to a certain extent. Of course, one is embittered, unreconcilable . . . vengeful even. A battle develops, a tug-of-war for the children, the property, the amount of alimony, child support. And the woman, at least in *our* so-called judiciary system, usually has the best weapons. They have been laid down by law. There have to be very, very considerable circumstances, for instance, for the woman *not* to get custody of the children. It's generally held that a child is worse off growing up without a mother, than without a father. And once she has the children, the rest sort of falls in line. The man almost always gets the short end of the stick and if he doesn't want to be in bondage for the rest of his life, he has only one way out . . . murder."

DeKok studied the man. He looked to be in his fifties, small, tubby and with a friendly, fleshy face. Slowly, the gray sleuth shook his head.

"You make dangerous statements," he cautioned.

Mr. Winepresser spread wide his arms.

"Obviously I'm not advocating that *any* man should kill his ex-wife. That's too absurd for words. I merely use the example in order to emphasize the absurdity of the burden placed on the ex-husband. It's based on a system of law that predates the middle ages. We're living in modern times. Women have long since been emancipated." He made a weary gesture. "But the man, the man will remain what he has been from the very first . . . her slave."

"Until death do us part," smiled DeKok.'

Mr. Winepresser snorted.

"Even then, she's still entitled to his pension, his life insurance policy, whatever."

DeKok leaned closer.

"Do you give lectures on the subject?"

"Yes."

"Don't you realize that there could be men in your audience who might . . . perhaps because they see no other way out . . . who just might follow your advice?"

Mr. Winepresser was visibly upset.

"I don't lecture to idiots," he protested sharply.

DeKok rubbed his face with his hands.

"Did you know," he said slowly, emphasizing the importance of the message, "that every one of the victims of what the papers are pleased to call the maniacal murderer . . . has been a divorced woman?"

There was a mocking smile on Winepresser's face as he looked at DeKok.

"Are you suggesting that I hold myself morally responsible for the murders?"

DeKok shrugged his shoulders as if the subject was of no importance.

"That, Mr. Winepresser, is strictly between you and your conscience."

* * *

From Heart Street they crossed Gentleman's Street toward Town Hall Street. It was busy in the streets. Behind them shimmered the outlines of the Wester Tower, the tallest steeple in Amsterdam. The structure dates from 1638 and was designed by Hendrick De Keyser, who also designed the South Church. De Keyser never saw the completion of his masterwork with the strikingly unusual upper galleries. He died long before the tower and most of the church was finished. The building was completed by his son. To DeKok the Wester Tower always seemed the demarcation between "his" Amsterdam and that which was built later. During the 17th Century the North, South and West Church had been built against what then had been the city walls. The East side of the old town was, of course, protected by the wide waters of the Amstel, the Ij and the harbors. Waters that today bisect the large city.

In front of them they discerned the gray walls of the Royal Palace which had originally been built as a Town Hall, long before the first Dutch king. Strange, thought DeKok, Holland had actually been started as a Republic, the Republic of the Seven United Netherlands and the U.S. Constitution was in large part based on the original Dutch Constitution. With the exception of ancient Rome, DeKok knew of no other country that had gone from a republican form of government to a monarchy.

Prins, who had been quiet up to now, broke into DeKok's thoughts.

"What exactly did you mean with the lowest common denominator for ex-wives?"

DeKok smiled.

"Well, I had a bit of trouble with that. I didn't really know how to express it. You see, as we know, Winepresser is divorced himself. Because of his activities, he comes in contact with a lot of divorced men. They write letters and tell him their tales of woe. Winepresser probably knows the problems like no other. You might say he's made a study of it. What I wanted him to do is give me an impression of the worst type of divorced woman, a woman who personifies all the bad, negative, irreconcilable attributes that is common in such a situation. In other words, the lowest common denominator."

"I understand," nodded Prins. "But what good is such an image, such a description?"

"I have a vague plan," answered DeKok. "I'm not yet sure how to put it in motion, if it is even possible to execute it." He stopped suddenly and pointed around. There was a determined

148

look on his face. "But I *will* rid this city of that maniac." It sounded like an oath.

Several pedestrians slowed down and looked at DeKok with surprise. But DeKok laughed. He had forgotten all about his tired feet. He almost skipped as he resumed toward his destination.

Prins followed, shaking his head.

* * *

Vledder was surprised and slightly insulted when DeKok and Prins entered the large detective room. He came from behind his desk and met them halfway.

"Did you go out with Prins?" he asked incredulously.

"Yes," nodded DeKok. "Prins informed me about a man who has been actively fighting for the rights of divorced men."

"And?"

"His battle continues," grinned DeKok pithily.

"But I was looking for you everywhere," complained Vledder. "The Commissaris wants to see you. He's been asking for you."

"When was that?"

"About half an hour ago."

DeKok calmly placed his coat and hat on the coat rack and walked out of the room. The Chief's office door was ajar. DeKok knocked politely and entered.

Commissaris Buitendam waved an elegant hand toward the chair next to his desk.

"Sit down, DeKok. How are you doing."

"Oh, I'm doing fine," answered DeKok blandly. "My feet hurt, but it's almost all gone now. For a while I thought I was catching a cold, but it was a false alarm."

The Commissaris smiled languidly.

149

"How droll," he said in his best upper-class accent. "I'm glad to hear you're in good health. But I was referring, of course, to your progress in the case of the women-killer."

"Nothing there," said DeKok, "progress I mean."

Commissaris Buitendam smiled thinly.

"You've been on the case for almost a week. There must be something to report, surely?"

DeKok scratched the back of his neck.

"You gave me a month, remember? And carte blanche."

Buitendam lowered his head.

"That's what I agreed to, I won't deny it. But the world is watching . . . and there's been an additional victim."

"You're talking about Josie Ardenwood?"

The Commissaris looked at some papers on his desk,

"Yes, that's her name."

DeKok nodded to himself.

"Sad," he said, "very sad." He watched his chief from behind narrowed eyes and made no further comment. He waited placidly.

"Well," said the Commissaris, after a considerable silence, "something better happen soon." There was annoyance in his tone of voice.

DeKok shrugged his shoulders insolently.

"Just tell me what you want to have happen," he said resignedly. "After all, I'm under your orders."

The commissarial face turned red.

"That's an uncalled for remark, DeKok," he said severely. "Surely you know that I cannot be expected to handle every case personally."

DeKok merely looked at him. He suddenly realized how arrogant the man was, how puffed up with his own self-importance. He was unable to see the man as he had been. His pose of disinterested severity was little more than thinly disguised fear . . . fear for what "they" would say, fear for his pension, fear to take a chance.

"And another thing, DeKok," continued the Commissaris, "I've received a complaint about you."

"Oh yes, who from?"

"Mr. Gellecom."

"Ah," sighed DeKok. "Did he complain in person, or did he use one of his influential friends to put the squeeze on me?"

"The complaint reached me via a superior officer," said the Commissaris ominously.

DeKok shook his head.

"Never heard of him," he said, a challenge in his voice. "Superior officer, I mean. I know a lot of good, hardworking officers, but superior . . . makes me think about the war . . . super-race and all that, you know." He continued in a conversational tone. "As I recall . . ."

The Commissaris interrupted him with an impatient gesture and DeKok looked at him with a question in his eyes.

"Mr. Gellecom states," declared Buitendam vehemently, "that you have interrogated his wife in an intimidating and indecent manner."

"Mr. Gellecom should be grateful he's still alive," snorted DeKok.

"What's the meaning of *that* remark, may I ask?"

"Oh, you may ask all right. But it means exactly what I said. Mr. Gellecom should be happy to get away with his life in the next few days."

"Get away from what?"

DeKok pressed his lips together, a stubborn look on his face.

Before the Commissaris could burst out in anger, the telephone rang. He picked up the receiver and listened. The blood drained from his face and then he replaced the instrument.

"It was for you," he said hoarsely. "Mr. Gellecom has just been placed in Intensive Care in Purmerend. The victim of an apparent heart attack." He looked at his subordinate and his eyes suddenly widened. "You knew that!" he accused. "You *knew* it was going to happen."

DeKok shook his head.

"You'll never know what I knew about it," he said grimly.

The Commissaris exploded.

"OUT!" he roared.

DeKok rose from his chair and left the room.

14

Vledder laughed out loud.

"Same old story again, I bet?" He looked, fondly at his partner. "I just knew that your last meeting was too cordial. It couldn't last."

DeKok leaned his head in his hands.

"I tell you, Dick, that man just rubs me the wrong way. And with each passing day I find him more obnoxious. It bothers me. I used to like him, well, accept him at least. But now . . . I don't know. I sincerely wonder if he knows anything at all about crime. He's only worried about his so-called dignity and his pension."

Vledder was not sure about his response. This was the second time in a week that DeKok had openly criticized the bureaucracy.

"Well," he began soothingly, "you have to . . ."

"That man makes me tired," interrupted DeKok sadly. "He's *still* not used to the fact that I have my own methods. He *knows* it, but he just refuses to accept it. There's no need to chase after me. If I catch the perpetrator, I'll bring him in. And then he can take all the credit . . . I don't care." It sounded cynical.

"Well," Vledder tried again, "in your own way you're just as . . ." Then he thought better of it. He reached behind him and handed DeKok an envelope.

"Here's a letter for you from a certain Mr. Winepresser."

DeKok took the envelope and carefully opened it.

"The lowest common denominator for a bad ex-wife," he grinned. "Old Winepresser is a man after my own heart. He works fast."

He gave the letter his full attention and then handed it to Vledder. The young Inspector read the lines. When he was finished, he looked at his partner.

"What's this?"

A mysterious smile appeared on DeKok's face and a gleeful, almost malicious light came into his eyes.

"If I'm right . . . a useful lesson for Diana Gellecom."

Vledder was confused.

"A lesson?" What do you mean?"

DeKok did not answer. He ambled over to the coat rack and made a grab for raincoat and inevitable decrepit hat.

"Come," he invited cheerfully, "we're off."

"Where to?"

"To Purmerend."

"What's in Purmerend?"

DeKok had a twinkle in his eyes when he answered.

"A man called Baantjer. He writes detective stories and even wrote an instruction manual for the police."

"What do we want with that guy?"

DeKok placed his hat squarely on top of his gray hair.

"Nothing," he chuckled, "not a thing. But there's also a hospital in Purmerend, a hospital with an Intensive Care Unit that is working very hard to keep Mr. Gellecom alive after he's been admitted for a heart attack."

"What!?"

DeKok nodded easily.

"I think it's only right that we should inquire after his health."

* * *

They parked the VW under the old beeches and walked up the circular driveway. Swans floated in a small pond in the center of the large, circular lawn enclosed by the driveway. To the left was a sign indicating out-patients and emergency rooms. They entered the main entrance of the hospital and stopped just inside the door. The lobby was deserted and the porter's lodge was empty. With a shrug they proceeded along the main corridor, looking for a nurse's station. The smell of floor polish and disinfectants was overpowering.

A door opened to reveal a pert nurse in a sparkling white uniform. DeKok addressed her.

"We're looking for a patient," he explained, "a Mr. Gellecom." His tone was humble, almost shy. "They told us he had been taken to Intensive Care . . . heart, you know." He made an apologetic gesture. "I'm sorry to be wandering around, but we're from out of town and don't know this hospital."

She smiled prettily and pointed.

"Around the corner, second door on the left. He's not in IC at all, he's in for observation."

DeKok bowed, holding his hat across his chest. The nurse took a step back, looked thoughtful and then smiled. Another conquest, thought Vledder enviously. DeKok could make himself loved, hated, or feared with a simple gesture. It was obvious that he had charmed the pretty little nurse with his old-fashioned courtesy.

The second door to the left opened up into a smallish room with a high ceiling. Gellecom seemed lost in the large, white bed. His eyes were closed and his heavy, horn-rimmed glasses were on a bedside table. He looked less impressive without his glasses.

DeKok coughed discreetly and the patient opened his eyes. He seemed surprised. His hand went toward the bedside table.

157

"Who are you?" he asked in an authoritative tone.

The gray sleuth gave him a winning smile.

"My name is DeKok," he said quietly, "DeKok with kay-oh-kay. This is my colleague, Vledder. We're police."

Gellecom looked searchingly at his visitors from behind his heavy glasses.

"*You* are Inspector DeKok?"

"At you service."

A hard look came into Gellecom's eyes.

"You bothered my wife."

"Did she complain personally?" smiled DeKok.

"No." Gellecom shook his head. "Mrs. Vries informed me about your outrageous behavior."

DeKok shrugged his shoulders and spread his hands.

"That doesn't mean a thing. Mrs. Vries was prejudiced. Therefore she drew the wrong conclusion."

"Diana fainted during your interrogation." There was no compromise in his voice, or his face.

DeKok looked serious.

"Your wife has gone through a difficult period in her life. A crisis. The sudden death of Professor Dinterloo has affected her severely."

Red spots appeared on Gellecom's pale cheeks.

"That fool," he hissed. "For some foolish reason she was very much taken with him. She even pursued him. Incredible!"

DeKok nodded to himself.

"Love is an incredible occurrence," he philosophized. "I understand that you have lost her love?"

Gellecom raised himself to his elbows.

"That's none of your damned business," he bristled.

DeKok regarded him with calm, understanding eyes.

"Exactly," he said, "and if you persist in addressing people this way, you'll never regain her love."

Gellecom sank back in the pillows.

"You came here to tell me *that*?"

DeKok smiled gently.

"Perhaps you'll find this hard to believe, but we came to inquire after your health."

Gellecom shook his head, a bitter smile around his lips.

"I don't think that your visit has been good for my health. You have shocked me, upset me severely, and me with a bad heart . . ."

DeKok waved away further complaints.

"Do not concern yourself. You'll be fine in just a few days. There's nothing wrong with your heart." He tapped his chest with a forefinger. "I mean the *pump* here . . . inside."

"Are you a doctor?" Gellecom asked belligerently.

"No, a cop . . . that's all."

He turned around and left the room without another word. Vledder, completely mystified, followed.

* * *

They walked back to the car. A storm was in the offing. The old beeches swayed and their crowns rustled in the strengthening wind. DeKok held on to his hat with one hand. Vledder looked at him.

"I thought you were rather reckless," shouted the young man in an attempt to be heard over the rising noise of the approaching storm. "I mean, the way you handled him. For a moment I thought he was going to have another heart attack." He laughed suddenly. "Then the fat would really have been in the fire . . . I can see it now. Large headlines in the papers: Without permission from attending physicians . . . cardiac patient dies during police grilling."

DeKok ignored his partner and continued his silent struggle against the strong wind. When they were in the car Vledder looked at the older man and placed both hands on the steering wheel.

"Where to?"

DeKok rubbed his chin pensively. He was wrestling with a problem. He needed complete assurance. Certainty concerning Gellecom's state of health. He could not afford to fail. His carefully thought-out plan had a good chance of being successful, but that all depended on the preparation. He now knew the secret of the naked lady and he wanted to make sure he could use it to his advantage. But he knew from bitter experience that people could only be manipulated so far, would only respond in the desired fashion if he firmly controlled *all* the variables. He pushed back his sleeve and looked at his watch.

"I have a friend, here in Purmerend," he said slowly. "A young physician and if I'm not mistaken, he'll be in his office about now."

Vledder grinned.

"You're going to have a physical?"

"Number five, Pan Flute Street," said DeKok evenly, ignoring the gibe. "It's on the other side of the railroad tracks . . . the neighborhood is called Corn Mill." He slid down in the seat. "I hope Jan is able to help," he murmured.

Three times they got lost. All streets in the Corn Mill neighborhood, a typical Dutch "new construction", looked alike. World War II had created a terrible housing shortage in the small, overpopulated country. The Dutch response had been typical. With the same boundless energy with which they tamed the sea, they had created entire cities on the outskirts of existing cities. The new suburbs, although comfortable and provided with all the necessary amenities, lacked the character and diversity of the pre-war construction. Streets looked alike with endless rows of houses, all the same, with standardized windows and doors, wide pavements and precise trees and shrubbery. The difference between one of these new neighborhoods and the inner city of Amsterdam, for instance, was as great as the difference between a well manicured English formal garden and a jungle. But still, mused DeKok, it had alleviated the housing shortage and most people did not mind, actually liked living in the sterile, painfully clean and neat neighborhoods. As they searched, DeKok thought with longing of the narrow alleys, tree-lined canals, quaint bridges and vibrant, vital chaos of his beloved Amsterdam.

They finally found Pan Flute Street and Vledder parked close to the curb. They left the car and walked toward number five. They stopped in front of the small, neat front yard, exactly the same size as all the other front yards. With exactly the same low, brick wall separating it from the pavement and from its neighbors on either side. They crossed the short gravel path toward the front door of the neat, yellow-bricked single family home. A small sign to the left of the door, just underneath the doorbell, announced: *J.C.A.M. Aken, Physician* and the consulting hours. As did most Dutch doctors, Dr. Aken kept consulting rooms in his residence. Few Dutch doctors have offices, other than in a hospital. But then, they also still make house calls.

A tall, good-looking nurse opened the door in response to their ring and showed them into a small waiting room. There were a few women, some with children on their laps. Vledder and DeKok sat down in silence and waited their turn. DeKok picked up an old magazine and idly glanced through the pages. He found a picture of a pastoral scene. A few cows huddled in the foreground of a large meadow, thick, threatening clouds gathering at the horizon. He became lost in the resigned dignity of the cows as they awaited the approaching storm. The photographer was an artist, concluded DeKok. He had almost perfectly captured a scene which had been painted almost four hundred year ago by Paulus Potter. He came out of his reverie as Vledder nudged him. It was their turn.

Doctor Aken looked shocked when they entered. Then he recognized the gray sleuth and came from behind his desk with outstretched hand.

"What a happy surprise," he said cheerily. "What are you doing in this neighborhood?" He had a marked southern Dutch, almost Flemish accent.

DeKok laughed happily. The warm greeting had lifted his spirits. He pointed at Vledder.

"This is Vledder," he introduced his younger colleague, "I've told you about him."

Dr. Aken shook hands with the young Inspector. His friendly face beamed.

"How did you wind up here? Police business?"

The gray sleuth sank down in the chair reserved for patients. The deep lines in his face were more prominent and there was a hopeful look in his eyes.

"I came to ask your personal assistance," he said.

The young doctor was surprised.

"*My* assistance?" he asked, confused. "Why me? I'm just a simple G.P. Not a specialist, no pathologist."

DeKok shook his head.

"I don't need one of those." He paused, looking for the right words. "In the hospital here," he said carefully, "there's a Mr. Gellecom. He's under observation for a suspected heart-attack. Apparently he was supposed to be in Intensive Care at first, but he's now just under observation. Whatever," he continued briskly, "that's as may be. I don't know who did the original diagnosis, but I think it's wrong." He sighed. "But even that doesn't concern me. As a matter of fact, I would prefer it if everybody, including Mr. Gellecom, kept thinking in terms of a heart attack. Although I'm convinced that there's nothing wrong with his heart, I want to be sure. I want a urine sample."

The young doctor smiled.

"But that's very easy. You just go to the hospital and ask for it."

DeKok shook his head.

"No, I can't do it that way. I'd need a warrant . . . red tape . . . official busybodies. And I simply have too few concrete facts and almost no grounds at all. I'll never get official permission and I don't want it, either. I want this to be between us. It's for me . . . eh, for my personal satisfaction. That's all. There's no intention, no matter how, to use it in a judicial way."

"And what do you want me to do?"

DeKok swallowed.

"Can you get me that urine sample?"

The young doctor blushed, played with his stethoscope.

"I'm not sure," he said hesitatingly, "which of my esteemed colleagues is the attending physician."

DeKok spread his arms in a gesture of surrender.

"I don't care how you do it. As long as it's Gellecom's urine. It should be easy for you. Don't you have hospital privileges?" He looked imploringly at the young physician. "You're not hurting anyone with it. That man's urine is just so much waste. But it would help me enormously."

Doctor Aken stared into the distance.

"What do you expect to find in the urine?"

"Colchicine."

The doctor looked startled.

"But that's a lethal poison."

DeKok nodded.

"Exactly right . . . a lethal poison."

* * *

163

The storm had grown to full strength as they drove back to Amsterdam. The waters of the North-Holland Canal showed whitecaps in the beams of the headlight and the road was just as wet from the canal water as from the rain. Here, where Holland's land reclamation projects had started, the ever-threatening waters seemed more menacing than usual. It was not just that the land was below sea level, everybody was used to that. But the very water table of the canal was below sea level and on a night like this the ancient dikes seemed too low, the windmills too frail and the ring canals outside the dikes seemed too narrow to keep the massive amounts under control.

With one part of his mind DeKok knew that an intricate system of windmills and more modern equipment was constantly being monitored and adjusted in order to make sure that Vledder could just discern the difference between canal surface and road surface. The wipers of the old car were in perfect order and swept water, leaves and even foam out of their field of vision with commendable haste.

Vledder peered through the windshield as he held the car on course. His actions were automatic, almost routine. His mind was primarily occupied with the case. There was a frown on his forehead and a brooding look on his face. As had happened so often before, he felt left out, an outsider looking in, as if he was not involved in the case at all. It made him moody, made him feel insecure and made him sad as well as irritated. He had known DeKok for many years and knew that the old man had obtained his "knowledge" from the same facts, remarks and circumstances that he, Vledder, had also seen and heard. Sometimes he thought he understood everything, that he actually had stolen a march on the old sly fox. But time and time again he learned, to his great sorrow, that DeKok had been just that one tiny step ahead of him all the time. No matter how much he admired and liked his old mentor, he could not help but be chagrined every time that happened.

He looked aside at the coarse, craggy face with the friendly expression of an old boxer, in perfect repose and with complete faith in the driving abilities of his young partner. Vledder knew every line of that familiar face. He felt a touch of tenderness in his heart and the feeling of dissatisfaction disappeared and made way for genuine regard.

"It took a while to convince your friend," remarked Vledder suddenly.

DeKok pushed his hat further back and looked incuriously out of the window.

"Jan is a nice guy and a good doctor. But I can understand how he feels. He's not used to conspiracies, not like us." DeKok chuckled. "After all, Rome wasn't built in a day. He'll come through. Tomorrow is soon enough." He pushed himself higher in the seat. "Sylvie Rebergen's apartment ... has that been released yet?"

Vledder shook his head.

"I think it's still sealed."

"Very good, in that case we'll make sure there's a new occupant tomorrow."

"A new occupant?"

"Exactly."

"Who?

"That, my dear boy, has to be a surprise for just a little longer."

Eventually they reached the station house and had to fight their way through a crowd in front of the desk-sergeant. About a dozen prostitutes were all declaring their innocence, or rights, at the top of their voices. Three uniformed cops stood at a distance and grinned as the sergeant tried to create some order in the chaos. Both Vledder and DeKok managed to get through the group of excited women and reached the comparative quiet of the restricted area of the station. As they made their way to the stairs, the sergeant managed to shout something at them above the noise.

"There's a guy waiting for you," he yelled.

DeKok lifted two fingers in acknowledgement and, followed by Vledder, climbed the worn out stone steps to the large detective room on the next floor. In front of the door to the detective room they found a large man with long arms and firmly planted legs as if he would deny anyone access to the room.

DeKok recognized him and approached, a smile on his lips.

"Good Evening, Mr. Rozeblad."

The man shook hands with the sleuth.

"I came to thank you," he said.

DeKok opened the door and motioned for the man to enter. When they had reached the desk at the far end of the room, DeKok invited Rozeblad to sit down while he moved behind his desk.

"Thank me for what?" asked DeKok.

"For the children, of course, it didn't take long to get them back."

"How are they adjusting to the death of their mother?" asked DeKok compassionately.

Rozeblad shrugged his shoulders.

"I don't think they really know. Lately they hadn't seen her often and I didn't allow them to view the corpse, of course. I don't think they've realized they'll never see her again. When they do, they'll be bit older and better able to deal with it."

DeKok nodded.

"It's always the children and innocent bystanders who get hurt, isn't it?" he asked rhetorically.

Rozeblad squirmed.

"I heard . . . that her friend . . . that's to say, her friend was also killed?"

"Josie Ardenwood." admitted DeKok.

Rozeblad squirmed some more and straightened his tie. Finally he seemed to gather enough courage to speak.

"Well, you see," he began slowly, "I . . . eh, I came really . . . I came to offer my help. You see, I've not always thought kindly about my wife. Perhaps she didn't deserve that. . . I don't know, that's just me . . . but . . . eh, she certainly didn't deserve what she got."

"Death?"

"Yes, death. She was, after all, the mother of my children . . . and . . . eh, I *did* love her at one time . . . very much." His eyes were moist. "Such a killer . . . such an animal . . . he should be found, *must* be found. That must be possible. He shouldn't be allowed to . . ." Rozeblad swallowed, did not complete the sentence. DeKok waited patiently.

"I know you guys are busy," continued Rozeblad after a while. "But I often have extra time on my hands. Perhaps I can find something out for you, shadow someone, be a look-out. You understand . . . sort of in her memory."

"A generous offer," said DeKok, feeling the man's pain and sympathizing with it. "I would very much like to take you up on it, but . . . my hands are tied. It's not allowed. In that respect I agree with the regulations. There are too many risks and my oath forbids me to endanger the lives of citizens. Also . . . now that their mother is gone, your children need you more than ever."

Rozeblad stood up.

"But I'm at your disposal. You know how to reach me."

DeKok nodded and shook hands. As Rozeblad turned to leave, DeKok asked him a question.

"Tell me Mr. Rozeblad . . . is Diana Gellecom good in karate?"

They left the office and walked deeper into the Quarter. As usual, the windows of the sex-shops drew a lot of attention.

"Strange guy, that Rozeblad," growled Vledder. "When his wife had just died, he wouldn't even hear about condolences. Now he seems ready to raise a monument in her memory."

DeKok waddled beside him. Despite his awkward seeming manner of locomotion, he had no trouble keeping pace with the tall, young man. He looked at Vledder.

"Did you call Mr. Hareberg, the lawyer?"

"Yes."

"And . . . is he going to be at Little Lowee's?"

"He'll be there within half an hour."

"He made no objections?"

"Lots," grinned the young Inspector. "He didn't have the time . . . it would be better if we met at his house . . . it was rather unusual . . . Lowee's bar is in such an unsavory neighborhood . . . more of that stuff."

"Then what?"

"Then I told him what you told me to tell him," laughed Vledder. "I told him exactly: *If you don't show up, DeKok will make sure that you'll be held accountable for the ten murders.* Then he capitulated."

They walked on in silence. Suddenly Vledder stopped and took DeKok by an arm. He leaned closer in the half-light and tried to read the old man's face.

"Can you do that?" he asked urgently.

"Do what?"

"Can you make him accountable for those murders?"

DeKok did not answer. He stared at the explicit scenes depicted on the posters outside Casa Erotica. His face was a steel mask.

15

It was beautiful summer weather. Storm and rain had been banished to a different depression area and a friendly sun stood high in a sky decorated with pure white cumulus clouds that floated like proud swans against the blue. A soft, cool breeze wafted along the galleries of the apartment building.

DeKok had no time for the view from the ninth floor. He stopped in front of number 784 and regarded the small, discreet nameplate with the name "sylvie rebergen', without capital letters. Young Vledder removed the police seals from the door and entered.

DeKok produced a small screwdriver and took down the nameplate. He replaced it with another, the same size. When he was finished he stepped back to gauge the effect. "Diana Gellecom," he read out loud and smiled a secretive smile.

Vledder came back outside and looked at the new nameplate.

"You really expect her?" he asked.

"Oh, yes. I stopped by this morning and told her everything I knew. She agreed whole heartedly."

"Just like that?"

171

"Not quite. She cried a lot. Diana Gellecom isn't at all the worldly, unfeeling woman one may suspect from her behavior. I really felt sorry for her this morning."

"Does Gellecom know . . ."

"He isn't supposed to know," said DeKok, shaking his head. "He would most certainly prohibit it . . . definitely interfere. And with Jan Aken's help, we'll keep him in the hospital for a few more days."

Vledder looked thoughtful.

"If she's going to be here tonight, we really should clear away some of the mess, inside. There's still blood on the carpet. Also, there are a lot of things that identify Sylvie. We should remove as many as possible."

DeKok nodded and sighed. He felt tired, strange and confused. Now that the drama seemed to approach its *denouement*, he was overcome by a general feeling of uncertainty. He was well aware of the risks he took and those that were taken by others. The responsibility weighed on him. He felt as if the burdens of the world had been placed on his shoulders.

The gray sleuth followed Vledder into the apartment and looked around. He realized it had been a mere seven days since they had walked in here for the first time, discovering Sylvie's mutilated corpse. It had been the beginning for them . . . the start of a week full of tempestuous developments. Did he really know the perpetrator? Would he come, tonight, to claim his eleventh victim? DeKok sighed again.

* * *

She arrived at exactly eight o'clock, a small overnight bag in one hand. She looked enchanting in a heliotrope pants suit with discreet, gold accessories and a gaily knotted white scarf of

172

exceptional dimensions. The golden hair cascaded loosely over the shoulders.

Fred Prins followed behind her. DeKok had planned for every eventuality and had sent Prins to Rijp to pick her up. Also, he wanted Prins involved. The young Inspector was big and strong and, he had learned much to his surprise, had for years been a devoted karate practitioner. Only this afternoon he had practiced for a full hour in the specific defense against the *shuto gammen-uschi*.

Greetings were stiff and formal and suffered from an almost tangible tension. Diana placed her bag on a nearby table and unwound her scarf. She came closer to DeKok.

"What time do you expect him?" she asked in a whisper.

"That's difficult to predict." DeKok made a vague gesture. "I suspect sometime between ten and eleven. He'll wait for total darkness. He certainly won't come sooner."

Diana Gellecom looked surprised.

"Then why are *we* here so early?" She looked around and her beautiful face fell. "I'm not all that enamored of the decor," she said in a bored tone, trying to hide her tension. "It's a chilly, almost sinister atmosphere," she added, revealing her true feelings.

DeKok nodded.

"But then," he said, "this is not exactly a social occasion. There wasn't much choice." His voice sounded unexpectedly hard.

She walked away from him. All three men admired the supple grace of her movements as she lowered herself into an easy chair.

DeKok looked at Prins and Vledder. With folded arms they leaned against the wall. Their faces were somber and in Vledder's case, slightly disapproving.

"We better go over everything one more time," said DeKok. "The biggest problem is that we can only offer limited protection to Diana. If the murderer isn't absolutely convinced that she's alone, he won't strike. Therefore, at least in the initial stages, Diana has only herself to depend on. According to VanLooijen, she should be able to resist to a certain extent, certainly enough to slow down any attacker. Prins, since he has the most recent experience, will go through the defense moves with her a few more times. Just to be sure. It's absolutely vital that the *nihon nukite*, the preliminary attack to the eyes, be neutralized at once."

DeKok fell silent. He rubbed his face with a broad hand. It was as if he suddenly realized to what dangers the young woman would be exposed. He hesitated. He had a strong urge to call it off. He wondered about the morality, the ethics, of using a young woman, anybody for that matter, as bait. What was more important, he wondered, the life of this woman, or catching the murderer. But, and DeKok was convinced on that point, if the murderer was *not* caught, the killings would continue. What was more important? Slowly he walked over to where she was seated. His face was serious as he squatted down next to her chair, bringing his eyes at the same level as hers.

"Diana," he said softly, "you can still refuse. Nobody will hold it against you."

She looked at him for several seconds. Her face was pale, but there was a dogged look in her eyes.

"No, DeKok, I won't back out. Not at this time."

DeKok rose with some difficulty. Despite his fitness report, he was no longer as limber as he used to be. He placed a fatherly hand on her shoulder and gave her an encouraging nod.

"Then I, too, will keep my word."

Her eyes were suddenly moist and for a moment it seemed as if her emotions would get the better of her. Then she recovered and a wan smile briefly touched her lips.

"You . . . eh, you may be assured of my gratitude." The words were regal, but the tone was that of a supplicant.

Fred Prins interrupted the private moment. He moved away from the wall and pointed at the door.

"What can we do if he lashes out at once? I mean . . . as soon as he's inside?"

DeKok spread wide his arms.

"I depend on the killer," he said. "I trust him." It sounded strange and cynical. Fred Prins did not hide his shocked surprise.

"Depend on the killer? Trust?" he protested.

DeKok nodded resignedly.

"Yes, I depend on his *modus operandi*, I trust he won't change his operating procedure, his standard pattern. Otherwise I would have never dared to do this. The killer never struck at once. All victims were found in their living rooms. And they were killed there. Most likely after a short, or longer, exchange of words. Diana will be relatively safe until she reaches the living room."

"And how do you know he won't come until after dark?" persisted Prins.

"A good question," smiled DeKok. He waved around the room. "In all cases the lights were still on when we discovered the bodies." He turned toward Vledder. "You read the files. It was like that in *all* cases, wasn't it?"

"You're right," agreed Vledder. "The lights were always on."

DeKok scratched the tip of his nose.

"None of the victims were found in night clothes. They were dressed for the street, or to receive visitors. If we combine those facts, we can deduce that the killer came after dark, but

175

before bed time. Between ten and eleven is then a reasonable assumption."

* * *

For more than two hours they had held more or less strategic positions. The apartment offered few possibilities for conceal-ment and it was, of course, vital to overpower the killer in time. Preferably in a compromising position, or after clearly declared intentions. They could not afford to leave any loose ends.

From where he was seated, DeKok had a reasonably clear view of the living room. They had rearranged the furniture to provide the clearest lines of visions. He could see Diana through the decorative glass of the hall door. She paced up and down with folded hands at waist height. Every once in a while she would throw back her head and shake loose her hair. Signs of great tension and nervousness.

A little further down the darkened foyer, closer to the living room, he heard Vledder's breathing. It was a sound he knew well. Together they had found themselves in this sort of situation before. DeKok hoped fervently that young Vledder would be able to control himself and would pick the right moment to intervene. Fred Prins would cheerfully assist in whatever action was taken. His joyful exuberance in his own strength and agility, made him a formidable ally. The time passed slowly. Minutes seemed like hours.

Suddenly the doorbell rang. Although they had expected it, the sound surprised them. DeKok looked through the clear parts of the glass and saw that Diana Gellecom had stiffened, frozen in position. He tried to project his thoughts at her, tried to telepathically impart her with the will and the strength to open the front door. Several seconds went by, then she stepped out of his field of vision. He listened intently and heard the clicking of

176

the lock. A man's voice, Diana's nervous answer. He could not discern the words. He listened to the tone ... the fear in the words that seemed to cut through his very soul.

The outside door closed and the door to the living room opened. Diana was again visible. She was facing a man of medium height, with round shoulders and long arms that made him look a bit dim-witted.

DeKok heard the tempo of Vledder's breath increase. He watched, tensely. The tableau of the man and woman in the living room was fixed indelibly on his retina. Two talking people. It seemed so peaceful, so everyday, so far removed from any criminal intent. Despite everything, he fleetingly doubted himself. Could he have been wrong, after all?

Then he saw the man take a step back and start to assume a position he had learned ... learned from VanLooijen's demonstrations. The living room door bounced open and Vledder rushed in. The man looked around, surprised. But only for a moment. Then he pushed Vledder aside and fled.

Suddenly DeKok's world seemed to move in slow motion. He watched as Prins floated into view, as the front door opened slowly, as if in a dream. He saw the man take a few steps to the railing that ran along the long gallery. His eyes opened wider as he saw the man jump, followed in an unreal, slow-motion ballet by Prins and Vledder. Slowly the man seemed to rise in the air and then disappear from view. With a shock, abruptly, everything reverted to normal speed as Prins and Vledder came to a sudden halt against the railing and then leaned far out into the night, trying to see a body that had already smashed against the ground below. From a distance he heard a loud, undulating scream and realized it came from Diana. He looked down and was surprised to discover her clutching the front of his coat.

DeKok placed a protective arm around the overwrought young woman and closed his eyes. In his mind he saw the drop, nine stories high, and he heard the sickening thud far below. He gently led Diana back into the living room and put her in a chair. He found a glass of water and held it for her.

Then he slowly walked out to the long balcony and joined Vledder and Prins who were still at the railing, stunned by what had happened and upset at their inability to prevent it.

DeKok placed a hand on each of the young shoulders. His voice was tired when he spoke. He had neither foreseen, nor desired this end.

"Call the paramedics," he said dolorously. "tell them to hurry. There are children in these apartments."

With bowed head he walked toward the elevators. Downstairs, outside, he shuffled toward the spot where he suspected he would find the corpse. He knelt down next to the inert form and felt for a pulse. The man was still alive!

Prins had come up silently.

"Do you know him?"

"Yes," nodded DeKok wearily, "Gajus Lyons ... Hareberg's senior clerk."

16

DeKok had invited them for an evening at his house. It had become a tradition, ever since he and Vledder had started to work closely together. In addition to Prins, he had also invited Robert Antoine Dijk, another young detective who, although not involved in this case, had often assisted Vledder and DeKok in the past. There were a number of loose ends that had to be discussed before Vledder could make the final reports. With a grateful sigh DeKok reflected that *that* was one of the chores that had been taken from him since Vledder and his computer had joined him. It was a difficult situation and Vledder would need all his ingenuity to concoct an acceptable report. The Commissaris had given him carte blanche ... within the confines of the law. And that was creating a problem. As far as DeKok was concerned, the law had little to do with justice and justice certainly could not always be found in the law books. In this case, too, he had applied his own kind of justice. He felt that Vledder and Prins would agree with him, but he worried nevertheless. Perhaps that was why he had also invited Dijk.

He picked up the bottle of fine cognac and poured generous measures in the waiting snifters while he looked at the three young men, one by one. They seemed ill at ease. There was tension and unrest in their eyes and he knew they had many questions. Vledder's right eye sported a large blue and yellow bruise where Gajus Lyons had hit him a glancing blow during his escape. The young Inspector felt the sore spot tenderly.

"That guy was so fast," he growled. "He hit me and was past me before I realized it."

DeKok replaced the bottle.

"Gajus Lyons is dead," he said evenly.

The three young men sat up straight and Mrs. DeKok, always present, but usually in the background, raised her eyebrows.

"Dead?" repeated Vledder and Dijk in unison.

"Dead?" echoed Prins, a second later.

DeKok nodded soberly, staring into his glass.

"In the end he went peacefully. Last night, morning actually, at around three o'clock. Perhaps it was better so, his chances were slim to none. It's a small miracle he survived the fall from the ninth floor. Almost every major bone in his body was broken and a number of organs were severely damaged. If he had hit concrete he would have been dead. The bushes and the grass cushioned his fall a little."

"Were you there?" asked Vledder.

DeKok stared into the distance, still not touching his glass.

"Together with his old mother," he said softly. There was a sad look in his eyes. "She was the only one with whom he still maintained some sort of contact. We sat next to the bed together when, after a labored confession, he closed his eyes for the last time and passed on."

"Did he confess to all the murders?" Dijk asked.

"Yes, all ten of them."

Prins was mystified.

"But why!?" he exclaimed. "What was the purpose of those killings?"

DeKok made a tired gesture with one hand. The other continued to cradle the snifter.

"Vengeance," he answered at last. "Or perhaps," he added, "you could say a . . . crusade."

"A crusade?"

Vledder thought he understood.

"Of course, a lone crusade against women who had ruined their husbands."

Fred Prins grimaced.

"Is that why he killed all those women?" There was disbelief in his voice.

DeKok raked his hands through his hair.

"I talked with his mother for a long time. A dear, sweet woman who was crushed to learn that her son would forever be known as a maniacal killer. Gajus Lyons was himself the victim of a woman who had deserted him and, through legal manipulations, had forced him into paying an exorbitant amount of alimony. There were two children and she managed to deny him visitation rights. She claimed he was a child-abuser and apparently she implanted that so strongly in the children's minds that they started to believe it. Although, as far as I've been able to check, there was never any confirmation of child abuse on his part."

"That excuse," said Mrs. DeKok, "seems to be used a lot, lately. Child abuse, I mean."

"Yes," answered her husband. "But we don't know, can't know . . . when it's true. We *do* know that it happens far more often than reported. Certainly too often to take lightly."

"Well," declared Dijk heatedly, "if it *does* happen, the abuser should be prosecuted. Was Lyons ever prosecuted for child abuse?"

"No," said DeKok. "But such is the current paranoia of our system. The accusation is enough. In many cases enough to deny even visitation rights to the alleged abuser."

"Never mind," interjected Vledder, "all child abusers should be castrated, sterilized and locked up for life."

"I agree with your sentiment," said DeKok, "but *not* without due process, *not* on just an accusation and most certainly *not* after having been pilloried in the press because of an accusation. That's not justice, that's mob rule."

"We digress," reminded Mrs. DeKok gently.

"You're right," agreed her husband. "As I said, Lyons was the victim of a harsh divorce settlement. He was a sensitive man for all that he was unbalanced and he could not live with the verdict. Especially, as far as we know, the unwarranted accusation of child abuse preyed on his mind. He developed a hatred for all women. He became a loner and avoided all social contacts. It's tragic that, in response to his mother's advice, he joined a club . . . a karate club. His mother had the best intentions . . . she observed her son's loneliness, his withdrawal, and wanted to get him back into the mainstream of life."

DeKok paused and closed his eyes. The other waited silently.

"Gajus Lyons," continued DeKok, "became an excellent student of karate. He went through the several grades faster than most and suddenly he realized his strength. I think *that* is when his plans took shape . . ."

DeKok did not finish the sentence. He lifted his glass and inhaled the aroma. Then he sipped with small, appreciative sips. The others followed his example and for a while nobody said anything as they savored the golden liquid.

Mrs. DeKok had meanwhile filled a sideboard with several platters of delicious food. She reached over and handed a platter to Dijk.

"Why don't you pass this around?" she suggested.

""With pleasure," answered Dijk. "Since it may be the last time I'll be able to do this."

"Why is that?" asked Mrs. DeKok, surprised.

"Dijk is leaving us," explained Vledder.

"Leaving the police?"

"Yes, he's taken a job with a large bank organization. I don't know what he'll be doing and he's a bit secretive about it. I think it's public relations."

"Well, I think he's eminently qualified for that," smiled Mrs. DeKok.

"I think the bank felt the same," laughed DeKok, "otherwise they would certainly never have hired him."

"In a way it's a pity," answered his wife. "Look at him. I like him. He's always so very polite and helpful and . . ." She paused, a twinkle in her eyes. ". . . he is, was that is, the best dressed cop on the force."

Dijk blushed. His cross had always been the continual teasing about his sartorial splendor. Mrs. DeKok patted his hand.

"Never mind, Robert, I do like the way you dress and I wish you all possible success in your new career."

Dijk thanked her.

Prins listened to the inconsequential prattle with mixed feelings. He was too restless to listen and too disinterested to participate. He leaned toward DeKok.

"At the time," he said, a bit irked, "at the apartment, when you knelt down beside him . . . you already knew who it was. You knew his name."

"Yes," admitted DeKok. "Gajus Lyons . . . Hareberg's senior clerk."

"How long did you know the killer?"

"You mean, how long have I known him, when did I first meet him?"

185

"No," said Prins impatiently. "When did you first suspect that he was responsible for the killings?"

DeKok made a nonchalant gesture.

"I think," he said thoughtfully, "that it must have been about two, three days ago that I first suspected it was Lyons."

"That long?"

DeKok smiled apologetically.

"There's many an obstacle betwixt suspicion and proof. It was not easy to overcome them."

Vledder grinned incredulously.

"We never said a word about Gajus Lyons . . . not one word . . . during the entire investigation," he exclaimed. "We just saw him that one time, when we went to visit Hareberg. He was the one in the hall that announced us, right?"

"Yes, so what?"

"So," challenged Vledder, "Where did you come up with that suspicion?"

DeKok waved defensively.

"Not so fast. Let's first get back to Sylvie's death . . . or rather, to the moment we found her mutilated body in her apartment. When we reported the find, the Commissaris immediately jumped to the conclusion that we had independently stumbled on the trail of the maniac. He, in order to cover himself, as well as to make some points, I'm sure, contacted the Chief Constable. The Chief Constable promptly 'rewarded' me with the entire investigation. Needless to say, I wasn't very happy about that. But now that the murders have been solved and the maniac stands before a heavenly judge, I'm equally sure that they are patting each other on the back and reassuring each other about what a smart decision they made." He paused, gestured pointedly. "But their conclusion was completely wrong. It was no more than coincidence that we happened to find the eighth

186

victim. Our investigation at the time had *nothing* to do with the killings."

"Oh, yeah," said Vledder. "and what about the Naked Lady?"

DeKok seemed embarrassed.

"I . . . eh, . . . I want to keep the secret of the Naked Lady just a little longer, until later. Then you will also hear how I have abused my authority, mis-used my position."

"Mis-used?"

"It'll keep," admonished DeKok.

Fred Prins cocked his head at the older man.

"The entire force was talking about it," he said. "Everybody felt that the Chief Constable had singled you out, might have wanted to put you on the spot."

"You mean, that after the special task force from Headquarters failed, they wouldn't have been too unhappy if I had failed as well?"

"Exactly."

DeKok shrugged his shoulders.

"That's the last thing I ever worried about. You know what they say about reputation . . . today's hero, tomorrow's bum. No, once I was reconciled to taking the case, I was only interested in finding the killer. And let's give credit where credit is due. Headquarters had used a lot of people to contact even more people and they had done an enormous amount of groundwork. You see," he digressed, "I've always been lucky . . . at least, that's the way I feel. But a lot of police work is grindingly boring. Usually covering the same ground, over and over. And the special task force had done that eminently well. They were very conscientious and very detailed and they followed up. Oh yes, they did," he told Vledder when he saw an unbelieving look in the young man's eyes. "Yes. the same evening that we had been assigned to the case, they had the courtesy to deliver the

187

complete file on the previous murders. Just because I didn't want to read the files, didn't mean I did not appreciate the courtesy. Vledder was a bit upset with me when I refused to read the files, as I remember."

"Well, you know . . ." Vledder did not go on.

"I understand," said DeKok. "But let me explain myself, if I may. In the past I have read a lot of those reports . . . reports by Headquarters, by special task forces. It's been my experience that their very completeness is so disheartening. After you read through everything you're left wondering in despair: *what's left for me to do*? Everything is done, all eyes dotted and all tees crossed, so to speak. And the last thing I needed at that time was to be discouraged. I simply didn't want to know how every lead led nowhere . . . how the investigations bogged down."

Vledder laughed.

"But you were mighty glad, at times, that I *had* read every word."

DeKok nodded approval.

"I was mighty glad of your assistance in this case . . . probably more than you ever suspected." He turned toward Prins. "From the very beginning I looked for a pattern . . . a pattern for the murders, a common thread, a hint that might give me some indication of the killer's thought processes. And it was Vledder who discovered the first hint. He is the one who discovered that all women were either divorced, or about to be divorced. From there we discovered that all the victims were the type of women who took unfair advantage of their ex-husbands. That was the first breakthrough that could be applied to all the victims. It was an important step, because there were no other similarities between the different women . . . apart from the fact that we could be reasonably sure that all had been killed by the same murderer."

"Yes," remarked Vledder, showing off his newly discovered knowledge of karate, "a *nihon nukite* followed by a *shuto gammen-uschi*."

"Therefore," resumed DeKok, "we established that the murderer had to know karate, at the very least had to know enough to be a master in the use of those two movements. Further he had to have a strong dislike, bordering on the psychotic, for divorced women. The big question remained, of course: How did he make his choice? There must be tens of thousands of divorced women in the country. Among them there *must* be a fair percentage who, let's say, take unfair advantage of their ex-husband, use divorce as a weapon." The gray sleuth made a helpless gesture. "I was caught, stuck, in a labyrinth of questions without any answers. That is ... until I turned the question around."

"Turned around?" asked Dijk.

"What do you mean?" asked Prins.

"Go on, Jurriaan," urged his wife, "we can do without the suspense."

DeKok looked shamefaced.

"Very well, my dear. But I had to pose the problem, before the solution can become intelligible. But I digress," he said hastily in response to a warning look from his wife.

"All right, then," he continued. "Instead of asking what determined the choice of the killer, I asked myself *how* was the killer able to make the choice? What was his data-base, as Vledder would say. What sort of information was available to the killer to enable him to make his choice." He laughed heartily. "And it was again Vledder who led me in the right direction. He discovered the eager Ms. Graven."

There was general surprise.

"The poor woman had nothing to do with it," Vledder sputtered.

"Of course not," agreed DeKok. "Why don't you send her some flowers in the next day or so, with our apologies. I'll happily pay for them. Especially since I was not exactly courteous during our interview. You see," he excused himself, "my mind ran away with an idea."

"What idea was that?"

"The idea that Ms. Graven would make an *ideal* suspect. She had all the facts that would enable her to make a choice. For a while I seriously considered if she could be the killer. If a woman could have killed so ruthlessly."

Vledder raised his arms and rolled his eyes.

"That's silly," he exclaimed. "I thought so at the time and I still think so."

DeKok ignored the interruption.

"Or, failing that, maybe somebody in her office, somebody who had access to the reports. Again I ran into a snag ... Although Ms. Graven had been in contact with a number of the victims, she had *not* been in contact with all of them. And that remained the essential, the crucial condition that had to be met, if I was ever to find the killer."

He paused briefly. Mrs. DeKok took the opportunity to urge a different platter of delicacies on the guests and Dijk, with the familiar ease of a favored houseguest, picked up the bottle and poured another round.

"What added to the confusion," resumed DeKok, "is that the killings followed each other at relatively short intervals. As far as that's concerned, the Commissaris was right. Speed was of the essence."

"For you, or for the killer?" asked Dijk.

"For me, actually. The sooner I found him, the sooner the killings would stop. The killer never was subject to time pressures. As I'll explain, each target was a target of opportunity."

"Some opportunity," sneered Vledder.

"I only mean it as a manner of speaking. Anyway, when we were checking the scene of Josie Ardenwood's death, Kruger, the fingerprint expert, told us that several times he had discovered the fingerprints of Hareberg, the lawyer. Kruger himself did not consider the discovery of particular significance. He mentioned it almost in passing. He also revealed that the special task force had interrogated Hareberg exhaustively and Vledder confirmed that. It was the considered opinion that Hareberg was merely the divorce lawyer and his presence in some of the houses of the murdered women was incidental. Frankly, I was perplexed and could not understand why no one had noticed it before." He paused and looked at the tense faces. "At that moment I knew *where* I could find the killer."

"In Hareberg's office," panted Vledder.

"Indeed, all the files concerning the divorcees were there readily available, complete with background details, addresses and other information. We know that Mr. Hareberg had an interesting sideline. He would select the best-looking women among his clients for sexual liaisons. The murderer selected his victims for death."

Prins moved restlessly in his chair.

"But you had come that far more than three days ago, two at least."

"Yes," nodded DeKok, "but as I said: *There's many an obstacle betwixt suspicion and proof.* How could I prove, prove without a shadow of a doubt, that the killer could be found in Hareberg's office? There certainly wasn't any proof to be gathered from the various crime scenes, although I knew very soon that Lyons had been studying karate. But, maybe because of him, there were a few other people in the office who *also* practiced karate. Gajus was the most likely candidate because he was a man, he was single and he was a loner. The only *sure* way was to set a trap for him, tempt him into committing another murder, so to speak."

"But how did you manage that?" asked Prins.

"By following the same procedure. The murderer, Gajus, if my suspicion were right, had gained his knowledge from the files in the office. Therefore it was matter of getting a file into that office that would attract the attention of the killer. The bait. And thanks to you, I had another brilliant thought."

"Mr. Winepresser?"

"Exactly. He extrapolated for me the lowest common denominator of a harridan, the worst possible example of a divorced woman."

Vledder looked thoughtful.

"As I remember, you said something about a lesson."

"Excellent, my boy, really excellent," praised DeKok. "A useful lesson for Diana Gellecom. Armed with Mr. Winepresser's guidelines, she went to see the celebrated divorce lawyer, the aforementioned Mr. Hareberg. She pretended to be the worst example of a divorced wife and requested the lawyer to start immediate divorce proceedings."

Vledder looked at him with admiration.

"That's why you insisted that Hareberg meet you at Little Lowee's!"

"Exactly," laughed DeKok. "I needed his cooperation. I had to take him into my confidence. After all, Hareberg was well acquainted with the Gellecoms and I couldn't run the risk that he might say something untoward, something that would give the plan away."

"He cooperated?"

"Eventually. Of course, like a true lawyer, he had all sorts of objections. In the end I promised him that in exchange for his cooperation I would remain quiet about his . . . eh, his escapades. Also, of course, I promised to destroy the fake file immediately afterward . . . immediately after the killer had been apprehended. In the end he had no choice."

Mrs. DeKok looked sharply at her husband.

"I can understand why the lawyer cooperated. You put him in an untenable position. On the one hand you blackmailed him with his affairs and on the other hand, if he did *not* cooperate, you could arrest him either for obstruction of justice, or as an accomplice in the murders."

"What?" asked Dijk. "How could the lawyer be an accomplice?"

"It's tenuous, I agree," answered DeKok. "But Gajus Lyons was his employee. His boss knew that I suspected Lyons. If he did *not* agree to help catch the killer, I would have arrested him as an accomplice, no doubt about that. If there had been an additional victim, I could probably have made it stick as well. At the very least he would not have enjoyed the publicity." He drained his glass. "But rest assured," he added grimly, "*if* another woman had been killed by Lyons, both Lyons and Hareberg would have gone to jail."

Mrs. DeKok felt he was hiding something. She knew her husband's stern opinions about right and wrong. She knew he never believed that a criminal, any criminal, operated in a vacuum. Something, or somebody almost always was the cause of criminal behavior. To root out the cause was DeKok's mission and his inability to do so was his greatest frustration.

"What about Diana?" she asked. "How did you get her to cooperate? Why would she expose herself to such a dangerous situation?"

DeKok evaded his wife's eyes and swallowed.

"Because," he said hesitatingly, "because . . . eh, . . . of the Naked Lady." He pointed at the bottle. "But first I need another drink."

"Remember what Lowee said," chided Vledder.

"What did that disreputable little man have to say?" asked Mrs. DeKok. She was no fan of Lowee.

"Eh," stammered Vledder ". . . nothing."

"He said," answered DeKok calmly, "that if one ever felt one *needed* a drink, it was a sure sign of alcoholism."

"Did he now?" queried Mrs. DeKok. "Well, Dick, you tell that barkeeper that my husband has never been drunk as long as we've been married. And if he enjoys cognac, I hope he'll enjoy it for a long time to come."

"Yes ma'am," answered Vledder, subdued.

"Now that that's settled," spoke Prins, "let me do the honors." He poured generous measures.

"And I'll get the coffee ready," interjected Mrs. DeKok. "Just to keep Lowee's mind at ease," she added jokingly.

"Lowee's right, you know," said DeKok. "Just because a person doesn't get drunk, doesn't mean he, or she, isn't an alcoholic."

Mrs. DeKok merely sniffed as she left for the kitchen.

The guests sipped their drinks in silence, a bit selfconsciously. But DeKok leaned back comfortably and enjoyed with full measure the aroma of the cognac, the feel of the glass, the interesting play of colors in the amber liquid and the taste of his favorite beverage. Drinking cognac, decided DeKok in silence, has nothing to do with alcohol.

"It's like watching a tall ship under full sail," he said, "and shrugging it off as transportation."

His audience was mystified. Only Vledder, more used to the ways of his partner, smiled and with a clear conscience took a large swallow of his drink.

When DeKok's wife returned with a tray, the three young men jumped up to help her. Soon coffee was passed around and the company settled themselves again to listen.

"First I want to defend my actions," began DeKok. "Plead, so to speak, for my behavior in this entire case. Please keep in mind that I had little choice. I would most certainly have failed using normal police procedures. Certainly I would not have been able to find the killer as quickly."

Prins waved away all excuses.

"The Naked Lady," he said impatiently, "who was she?"

DeKok shook his head sadly. It hurt him a bit that nobody seemed to be interested in his excuses, his justifications.

"Let's get back to the Tropic Oil night in Casa Erotica." he said weakly. "The night that Dinterloo had an argument with Gellecom. It wasn't a coincidental outburst. Dinterloo felt threatened. He could not handle the many intrigues at the top of the organization. In addition he was being pursued by Diana Gellecom who said she was in love with him and wanted to marry him. She urged him repeatedly to get a divorce. When Dinterloo observed that there was still a *Mister* Gellecom, Diana told him without any scruples that it would be easy to get rid of him and she told him how . . . by using the naked lady."

He paused and closed his eyes as if to focus his thoughts. Vledder was just about ready to urge him on when he continued.

"Dinterloo panicked. Despite his great intellect, he was not able to cope with the everyday vagaries of life. In order to safeguard the future of his wife and child, he bought a substantial insurance policy . . . and he wrote his own death announcement. Still contemplating suicide, he drank to excess that night at Casa Erotica until Sylvie Rebergen took pity on him and took him home to her apartment. That is where the drunk Professor Dinterloo revealed everything about himself, about Diana Gellecom and . . . about the naked lady."

"Now we're getting somewhere," observed Prins with satisfaction.

"Sylvie," resumed DeKok, "was no more than a sweet little whore for men with lots of money. I mean to say, her interests and education were limited. She probably listened to Dinterloo with feigned interest and sympathy and more than likely didn't understand a word. The next morning Dinterloo told his wife all about Sylvie, that sweet little girl who had shown so much understanding and gave her the address."

"He did?" Mrs. DeKok was astounded.

"Yes," answered DeKok absent-mindedly. Then, more briskly, he went on: "Two days later, returning from Diana's home, Dinterloo committed suicide by driving into the canal, making it look like an accident. His policy would pay double indemnity in case of accidental death, you see. And nothing in case of suicide. As we know, the suicide was ruled an accident and who are we to argue. In any case, Mrs. Dinterloo dutifully circulated the death announcements so thoughtfully provided by her husband. She also sent one to Sylvie. And that was for us the start of the drama. Sylvie was shocked and surprised by the quick death of the man she had known for just a few days. She was puzzled. She remembered fragments of the conversation that night, about victims, a naked lady and, with the help of Little Lowee, got the information to me. Before I had a chance to ask her what was the purpose, she was killed."

Prins spread wide his arms.

"But what about the naked lady, how did you discover her?"

DeKok smiled.

"You show evidence of a one-track mind, my boy," he said.

Prins squirmed.

"Well, I . . . eh, I just want to know."

"And so you shall. The first hint came from Dinterloo himself . . . in his death announcement. It was a macabre joke, clearly meant for Diana Gellecom. Remember what it said in the circular: *At the request of the deceased: no crocuses, or other flowers*. A strange request with an obvious emphasis on crocuses. I was at a complete loss and had no idea what to think of it . . . until we talked to Gellecom's driver in Rijp. He said something that struck me as we admired the magnificent garden. He said that Madame, an obvious reference to Diana, was even able to grow crocuses in the fall."

"Crocuses in the fall?" Prins was taken aback. Like most Dutch people he knew something about bulb flowers. The Dutch grow and export more flower bulbs than all the rest of the world combined. Every kid grows at least one bulb while in first or second grade. The procedure is always the same. The bulbs are stored in a dark closet until late winter. Then they are placed in a special vase that allows just the bottom of the bulb to be moistened and after the roots appear, the entire class will joyfully plant the bulbs in the school yard and wait for the flowers to come up. Clearly Fall is *not* the time to grow flower bulbs.

DeKok, aware of what went through the young man's mind, nodded slowly. He raised a finger in the air.

"Again there was mention of crocuses," he said, "crocuses in the Fall. At first the significance escaped me, but I did decide to check it out. The experts I consulted were quite positive: crocuses do *not* flower in the Fall. But there is a bulb-like flower that does. The root resembles a bulb, the purple flower resembles a crocus and it's commonly called a Naked Lady."

"So what?" asked Prins, disappointed. "What's so special about that?"

"Very much," assured DeKok didactically. "As I said, the plant flowers in the Fall. It is a so-called radical growth, that is, the leaves originate in the root, grow from the root, leaving the stem bare . . . naked, you see. That's part of the reason it's called a Naked Lady. The Latin name is *Colchicum autumnale*, named after Medea of Colchis, a renowned poisoner and sorceress of ancient legends."

"Poison?"

"Exactly. Colchicine, a deadly poison that Diana Gellecom grew in her garden for just one purpose ... to get rid of her husband if that happened to become necessary."

Vledder could contain himself no longer. He rose from his chair and his voice was agitated.

"She did it," he exclaimed heatedly, "Damn ... eh, darn if she didn't." People would try to avoid strong language around DeKok and Vledder remembered, even in his excitement. Mrs. DeKok smiled indulgently. She was known to be more tolerant in that respect. And Vledder was one of her favorites.

"Yes, she did," answered DeKok. "Diana Gellecom loved a challenge. It was a passion that drove her. She must have suspected I knew too much about the Naked Lady, but yet she administered colchicine to her husband, in a whiskey she poured for him in order to toast his safe return from the United States."

"What a bitch," hissed Prins. He noticed DeKok's look and hastily added, "Sorry ma'am."

Mrs. DeKok nodded seriously.

"I feel the same way," she said with indignation in her voice. Vledder was otherwise occupied.

"You didn't arrest her?" he asked, wondering.

DeKok shook his head.

"No, I went to Rijp with the urine sample. Then I told her that she had made an attempt on her husband's life. I showed her the bottle and told her that laboratory results clearly indicated the presence of colchicine in the system. Then I mentioned, casually, that I *could* just drop the bottle and let it shatter if ... if, she was prepared to give me her cooperation in unmasking the killer."

Mrs. DeKok was visibly upset.

"But that's blackmail ... the second time ... just plain blackmail. How mean ... how, how reprehensible."

DeKok squirmed a bit under the onslaught, but did not back down.

"You're absolutely right. It's even worse than that ... endangerment, entrapment ... and the Criminal Code mentions specific prohibitions against it. But ... without her testimony it'll be hard to prove."

Mrs. DeKok was not reconciled.

"How could you do it?"

"I wanted to start off with an excuse, a pleading ... pleading my case, I mean. But none of you wanted to listen to my justification. I used my knowledge of the Naked Lady, mis-used as I tried to say, to force Diana Gellecom to cooperate. I used my official position to put pressure on Mr. Hareberg. It's all true. In Diana's case I definitely put her in harm's way, there's no question about it. If there had been, Jan VanLooijen would have soon disabused me of that idea. Lyons was an expert in karate and Diana, even prepared, would have had only one chance in ten of defending herself successfully. And there was no way *we* could adequately protect her."

Prins snorted.

"Is she going to divorce her husband, after all that has happened?"

"No," answered DeKok. "I mentioned a 'lesson' for Diana. In the course of our preparations she had a good opportunity to study the fake file, the file that described 'the lowest common denominator' of a vengeful ex-wife. She must have had second thoughts about her own attitude to marriage. Be that as it may," he added with a grin, "earlier tonight she was at the Purmerend hospital and with loving care she helped put her husband in the Rolls and took him home."

Vledder looked suspicious.

"What about the urine sample?" he wanted to know.

DeKok made an apologetic gesture.

"I was careless. It happened to drop out of my hand, just as I was crossing a tile floor. It was no use to obtain another sample. Gellecom's kidneys had meanwhile done their job and filtered all the poison out of his system."

"Oh, yes? What about the lab analysis?"

"There never was a lab analysis," answered DeKok and he grinned mischievously.

17

A slow, sluggish rain descended from a low, melancholy sky. The clouds were so low and seemed so solid they looked like they were anchored for the duration and would never leave again. As if it would rain in Amsterdam until the end of time.

DeKok pulled up the collar of his raincoat and pulled his old, felt hat deeper in his eyes. In his typical, ambling gait he waddled across the gravel of the cemetery. The water dripped down his chin and under his collar. His shoes made squishy sounds as he walked. Gajus Lyons was being buried. DeKok wanted to attend, partly from piety and also because of a vague feeling of guilt, guilt for his untimely death.

The cemetery looked sad and deserted. The flowers seemed to have lost all color and the birds were sheltering against the rain. Head down, hands deep in his pockets, DeKok strode on. When he looked up he saw a woman in the distance. Lonely and alone she tried to shelter under the portico of the Chapel.

When he came closer he smiled in recognition.

"Mother Lyons," he exclaimed. "What are you doing here?"

"I'm waiting for him," she said simply, looking up at him.

"You're alone?"

She nodded. The water ran down the brim of her hat.

"Yes, I came by streetcar."

DeKok shook his head in irritation.

"You should have insisted . . . you should have come with the casket, a car should have been provided."

She lowered her head.

"They asked, but I refused."

DeKok looked at her searchingly.

"But why?" he asked, although he suspected the answer.

She sighed.

"The shame of it all, the scandal. Everybody knows him now, knows who he is . . . was."

DeKok pressed his lips together and quickly suppressed an angry look. Gently he took her chin in his hand and forced her to look at him.

"He was your child, wasn't he? Would you deny him, even after death?"

A tear came into her eyes and quickly mixed with the rain on her cheeks. She placed her head against his chest and sobbed.

A large hearse arrived with unseemly speed. With screeching brakes it stopped in front of the Chapel, spraying gravel in all directions. A man stepped out and dashed across the intervening space, protecting his head with a newspaper.

"Are you here for Mr. Lyons?"

DeKok nodded.

"Oh," said the man, visibly disappointed. Apparently he had not expected anybody. "You may follow us," he said and darted back to the car. After a few seconds the car moved off at a walking pace.

Mother Lyons and DeKok followed behind the car as it wended its way to the grave site. The gleaming hearse made no sound and seemed to float in front of them as if carried on the wind and the backsplash of the rain. After about ten minutes the car stopped. They looked past the car and discovered a woman

204

and two children waiting at the grave site. DeKok felt the older woman press herself against him. With concern he looked aside.

"Who is she?" he asked softly.

"Her."

"Who?"

"Marie . . . the woman who was married to Gajus . . . his ex, his ex-wife."

"And their children?"

She nodded.

DeKok suddenly felt her stiffen.

"What's she doing here?" she hissed. "Why is she here? There's nothing to find here . . . it's got nothing to do with her, not now, not anymore."

DeKok pulled her back out of sight, behind the hearse. His face was serious.

"Hate," he said evenly, "is a disease. It killed your son."

She looked at him. DeKok watched as the harsh expression on her face slowly softened, how his words seemed to penetrate. She pulled herself loose and shuffled past the car toward the gaping hole in the ground. From a distance the gray sleuth watched her greet the waiting woman and children. He watched as the children each took a hand and stood next to her.

He turned around. He had not come for a confrontation. He did not want to see the face of the young woman, the bright little faces of the children. Gajus Lyons was dead and he had been wrong.

Alone and with a strange, empty feeling in the pit of his stomach he left the cemetery. Outside the gate Vledder waited with the old VW. Without a word he climbed in the car and sat down. Vledder took one quick look at his face and remained silent.

The car bounced away from the curb in the wrong gear.

What Others Say About Our Books
(a sampling of critical reviews provided by our readers)

About BAANTJER, the author of the "DeKok" books: The Reader's Digest has already used seven books by Baantjer in *Het Beste Boek* (Best Books), to great enjoyment of our readers (*L.C.P. Rogmans,* **Editor-in-Chief, [Dutch] Reader's Digest**); A Baantjer book is checked out of a library more than 700,000 times per year (**Netherlands Library Information Service**); We have to put the second printing of his books on press before the first printing has even reached the bookstores, no matter how many we print (*Wim Hazeu,* **Baantjer's Dutch Publisher**); The style reminds me a bit of Georges Simenon. Fast, clever and satisfying (*Lucinda May,* **Mysteries by Mail**).

MURDER IN AMSTERDAM, the two very first "DeKok" stories for the first time in a single volume, containing *DeKok and the Sunday Strangler* and *DeKok and the Corpse on Christmas Eve.* (ISBN 1-881164-00-4): If there could be another Maigret-like police detective, he might well be Detective-Inspector DeKok of the Amsterdam police. Similarities to Simenon abound in any critical judgement of Baantjer's work (*Bruce Cassiday,* **International Association of Crime Writers**); The two novellas make an irresistible case for the popularity of the Dutch author. DeKok's maverick personality certainly makes him a compassionate judge of other outsiders and an astute analyst of antisocial behavior (*Marilyn Stasio,* **The New York Times Book Review**); Both stories are very easy to take (**Kirkus Reviews**); Inspector DeKok is part Columbo, part Clouseau, part genius, and part imp. Baantjer has managed to create a figure hapless and honorable, bozoesque and brilliant, but most importantly, a body for whom the reader finds compassion (*Steven Rosen,* **West Coast Review of Books**); Readers of this book will understand why the author is so popular in Holland. His DeKok is a complex, fascinating individual (*Ray Browne,* CLUES: **A Journal of**

Detection); This first translation of Baantjer's work into English supports the mystery writer's reputation in his native Holland as a Dutch Conan Doyle. His knowledge of esoterica rivals that of Holmes, but Baantjer wisely uses such trivia infrequently, his main interests clearly being detective work, characterization and moral complexity **(Publishers Weekly).**

DEKOK AND THE SOMBER NUDE (ISBN 1-881164-01-2): It's easy to understand the appeal of Amsterdam police detective DeKok; he hides his intelligence behind a phlegmatic demeanor, like an old dog that lazes by the fireplace and only shows his teeth when the house is threatened (*Charles Solomon,* **Los Angeles Times**); A complete success. Like most of Baantjer's stories, this one is convoluted and complex **(CLUES: A Journal of Detection);** Baantjer's laconic, rapid-fire storytelling has spun out a surprisingly complex web of mysteries **(Kirkus Reviews).**

DEKOK AND THE DEAD HARLEQUIN (ISBN 1-881164-04-7): Baantjer's latest mystery finds his hero in fine form. As in Baantjer's earlier works, the issue of moral ambiguity once again plays heavily as DeKok ultimately solves the crimes **(Publishers Weekly);** Real clarity and a lot of emotional flexibility **(Scott Meredith Literary Agency);** DeKok has sympathy for the human plight and expresses it eloquently. *(Dr. R.B. Browne,* **Bowling Green State University).**

DEKOK AND THE SORROWING TOMCAT (ISBN 1-881164-05-5): The pages turn easily and DeKok's offbeat personality keeps readers interested **(Publishers Weekly);** Baantjer is at his very best. There's no better way to spend a hot or a cold day than with this man who radiates pleasure, adventure and overall enjoyment. A ***** (five stars) rating for this author and this book **(CLUES: A Journal of Detection).**

DEKOK AND THE DISILLUSIONED CORPSE (ISBN 1-881164-06-3): Baantjer has provided a fine and profound series of books **(Popular Press);** Baantjer seduces mystery lovers. "Corpse" titillates with its unique and intriguing twists on a familiar theme (*Rapport,* **The West Coast Review of Books**).

DEKOK AND THE CAREFUL KILLER (ISBN 1-881164-07-1): DeKok is ever interesting, a genuine "character". More descriptive, however, is the compassion in DeKok's heart (**CLUES: A Journal of Detection**); This is entertaining reading (**Rapport**).

DEKOK AND THE ROMANTIC MURDER (ISBN 1-881164-08-X): A clever false-suspicion story. Everyone should read these stories (**CLUES: A Journal of Detection**); For those of you already familiar with this loveable old curmudgeon, you're sure to enjoy this installment. Score one for the Dutch (*Dorothy Sinclair,* **The Crime Channel**).

DEKOK AND THE DYING STROLLER (ISBN 1-881164-09-8): An intriguing story about youth and violence (**CLUES: A Journal of Detection**).

DEKOK AND THE CORPSE AT THE CHURCH WALL (ISBN 1-881164-10-1): Detective-Inspector DeKok returns in another solid offering from Baantjer (**Publishers Weekly**); Has enough red herrings to keep the most sophisticated expert guessing (**Rapport**); DeKok is a careful, compassionate policeman in the tradition of Maigret; crime fans will enjoy this book (**Library Journal**).

DEKOK AND THE DANCING DEATH (ISBN 1-881164-11-X): No reviews received at press time.

DEKOK AND THE NAKED LADY (ISBN 1-881164-12-8): This is the twelfth book about DeKok and his assistant, Vledder. This time it also means an even dozen murders. Baantjer spins his usual entertaining yarn (**Publishers Weekly**).

DEKOK AND MURDER ON THE MENU (ISBN 1-881164-31-4) by Baantjer: One of the most successful achievements. DeKok has an excellent sense of humor and grim irony (**CLUES: A Journal of**

Detection); Terrific on-duty scenes and dialogue, realistic detective work and the allure of Netherlands locations (**The Book Reader**).

What others say about ELSINCK:

About **TENERIFE!** (ISBN 1-881164-51-9) by Elsinck: A swiftly paced, hardhitting story. Not for the squeamish. But nevertheless, a compelling read, written in the short take technique of a hard-sell TV commercial with whole scenes viewed in one- and two-second shots, and no pauses to catch the breath (*Bruce Cassiday,* **International Association of Crime Writers**); A fascinating work combining suspense and the study of a troubled mind to tell a story that compels the reader to continue reading (*Mac Rutherford,* **Lucky Books**); This first effort by Elsinck gives testimony to the popularity of his subsequent books. This contemporary thriller pulls no punches. A nail-biter, full of European suspense (**The Book Reader**); . . . A wonderful plot, well written—Strong first effort—Promising debut—A successful first effort. A find!—A well written book, holds promise for the future of this author—A first effort to make dreams come true—A jewel of a thriller!—An excellent book, gripping, suspenseful and extremely well written . . . (**A sampling of Dutch press reviews**).

About **MURDER BY FAX** (ISBN 1-881164-52-7) by Elsinck: Elsinck has created a technical tour-de-force. This high-tech version of the epistolary novel succeeds as the faxed messages quickly prove capable of providing plot, clues and characterization (**Publishers Weekly**); This novel by Dutch author Elsinck is so interestingly written it might be read for its creative style alone. It is sharp and concise and one easily becomes involved enough to read it in one sitting. MURDER BY FAX cannot help but have its American readers fall under the spell of this highly original author (*Paulette Kozick,* **West Coast Review of Books**); This clever and breezy thriller is a fun exercise. The crafty Dutch author peppers his fictional fax copies with clues and red herrings that make you wonder who's behind the scheme. Elsinck's spirit of inventiveness keeps you guessing up to the satisfying end

(*Timothy Hunter,* [Cleveland] **Plain Dealer**); The use of modern technology is nothing new, but Dutch writer Elsinck takes it one step further (*Peter Handel,* **San Francisco Chronicle**); . . . Riveting—Sustains tension and is totally believable—An original idea, well executed—Unorthodox—Engrossing and frightening—Well conceived, written and executed—Elsinck sustains his reputation as a major new writer of thrillers . . . (**A sampling of Dutch press reviews**).

About **CONFESSION OF A HIRED KILLER** (ISBN 1-881164-53-5) by Elsinck: Elsinck saves a nice surprise, despite its wild farrago of murder and assorted intrigue (**Kirkus Reviews**); Elsinck remains a valuable asset to the thriller genre. He is original, writes in a lively style and researches his material with painstaking care (*de Volkskrant,* **Amsterdam**).